D0732396

WILLIAM HENRY HUDSON

W. H. Hudson was born on the 4th of August 1841 at Quilmes in the province of Buenos Aires in the Argentine Republic. His parents were emigrants to the Argentine from New England. Hudson went to England (one of his grandparents was English) in 1874 and never returned to the land of his birth. He married Emily Wingrave, a singer, music teacher and boarding-house keeper, and the couple lived for many years in poverty and obscurity in London.

His first book, *The Purple Land that England Lost*, was published in 1885 (revised and republished as *The Purple Land* in 1904), and was followed during the next thirty-five years by *Idle Days in Patagonia* (1893); *Birds and Man* (1901); *Tales of the Pampas* (1902); his classic novel, *Green Mansions* (1904); *Far Away and Long Ago* (1918); *The Book of a Naturalist* (1920); and others.

After living most of his life off a public pension, in his closing years, owing to the growing fame and sale of his books, Hudson was able to be the sole support of his family. He died in London on the 18th of August 1922.

Yours sincerely
W. H. Hudson

TALES
OF THE PAMPAS

BY
W. H. HUDSON

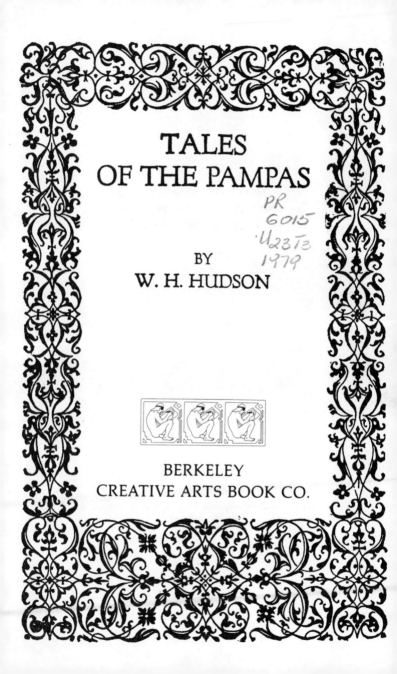

BERKELEY
CREATIVE ARTS BOOK CO.

Published by Creative Arts Book Company/833 Bancroft Way/Berkeley, California 94710
ISBN 0-916870-23-5

CONTENTS

EL OMBÚ

EL OMBÚ

This history of a house that had been was told in the shade, one summer's day, by Nicandro, that old man to whom we all loved to listen, since he could remember and properly narrate the life of every person he had known in his native place, near to the lake of Chascomus, on the southern pampas of Buenos Ayres.

IN all this district, though you should go twenty leagues to this way and that, you will not find a tree as big as this ombú, standing solitary, where there is no house; therefore it is known to all as *"the* ombú," as if but one existed; and the name of all this estate, which is now ownerless and ruined, is El Ombú. From one of the higher branches, if you can climb, you will see the lake of Chascomus, two thirds of a league away, from shore to shore, and the village on its banks. Even smaller things will you see on a clear day; perhaps a red line moving across the water— a flock of flamingos flying in their usual way. A great tree standing alone, with no house near it; only the old brick foundations of a house, so overgrown with grass and weeds that you have to look closely to find them. When I am out with my flock in the summer time, I often come here to sit in the shade. It is near the main road; travellers, droves of cattle, the diligence, and bullock-carts pass in sight. Sometimes, at noon, I find a traveller resting in the shade, and if he is not sleeping we talk and he tells me the news of that great world my eyes have never seen.

They say that sorrow and at last ruin comes upon the house on whose roof the shadow of the ombú tree falls; and on that house which now is not, the shadow of this tree came every summer day when the sun was low. They say, too, that those who sit much in the ombú shade become crazed. Perhaps, sir, the bone of my skull is thicker than in most men, since I have been accustomed to sit here all my life, and though now an old man I have not yet lost my reason. It is true that evil fortune came to the old house in the end; but into every door sorrow must enter—sorrow and death that comes to all men; and every house must fall at last.

Do you hear the mangangá, the carpenter bee, in the foliage over our heads? Look at him, like a ball of shining gold among the green leaves, suspended in one place, humming loudly! Ah, señor, the years that are gone, the people that have lived and died, speak to me thus audibly when I am sitting here by myself. These are memories; but there are other things that come back to us from the past; I mean ghosts. Sometimes, at midnight, the whole tree, from its great roots to its topmost leaves, is seen from a distance shining like white fire. What is that fire, seen of so many, which does not scorch the leaves? And, sometimes, when a traveller lies down here to sleep the siesta, he hears sounds of footsteps coming and going, and noises of dogs and fowls, and of children shouting and laughing, and voices of people talking; but when he starts up and listens, the sounds grow faint, and seem at last to pass away into the tree with a low murmur as of wind among the leaves.

As a small boy, from the time when I was able, at the age of about six years, to climb on to a pony and ride, I knew this tree. It was then what it is now; five men with their arms stretched to their utmost length could hardly encircle it. And the house stood there, where you see a bed of nettles—a long, low house, built of bricks, when there were few brick houses in this district, with a thatched roof.

The last owner was just touching on old age. Not that he looked aged; on the contrary, he looked what he was, a man among men, a head taller than most, with the strength of an ox; but the wind had blown a little sprinkling of white ashes into his great beard and his hair, which grew to his shoulders like the mane of a black horse. That was Don Santos Ugarte, known to all men in this district as the White Horse, on account of the whiteness of his skin where most men look dark; also because of that proud temper and air of authority which he had. And for still another reason—the number of children in this neighborhood of which he was said to be the father. In all houses, for many leagues around, the children were taught to reverence him, calling him "uncle," and when he appeared they would run and, dropping on their knees before him, cry out *"Bendicion mi tio."* He would give them his blessing; then, after tweaking a nose and pinching an ear or two, he would flourish his whip over their heads to signify that he had done with them, and that they must quickly get out of his way.

These were children of the wind, as the saying is, and the desire of his heart was for a legitimate son, an Ugarte by name, who would come after him at El Ombú, as he had come after his father. But though he had married thrice, there was no son born, and no child. Some thought it a mystery that one with so many sons should yet be without a son. The mystery, friend, was only for those who fail to remember that such things are not determined by ourselves. We often say, that He who is above us is too great to concern Himself with our small affairs. There are so many of us; and how shall He, seated on his throne at so great a distance, know all that passes in his dominions! But Santos was no ordinary person, and He who was greater than Santos had doubtless had his attention drawn to this man; and had considered the matter, and had said, "You shall not have your desire; for though you are a devout man, one who gives freely of his goods to the church and my poor, I am not wholly satisfied with you." And so it came to pass that he had no son and heir.

His first two wives had died, so it was said, because of his bitterness against them. I only knew the third—Doña Mericie, a silent, sad woman, who was of less account than any servant, or any slave in the house. And I, a simple boy, what could I know of the secrets of her heart? Nothing! I only saw her pale and silent and miserable, and because her eyes followed me, I feared her, and tried always to keep out of her way. But one morning, when I came to El Ombú and went into the kitchen, I found her there alone, and before I could escape she caught me in her arms, and lifting me off my feet strained me against her breast, crying, *hijo de mi alma,* and I knew not what beside; and calling God's blessing on me, she covered my face with kisses. Then all at once, hearing Santo's voice without, she dropped me and remained like a woman of stone, staring at the door with scared eyes.

She, too, died in a little while, and her disappearance made no difference in the house, and if Santos wore a black band on his arm, it was because custom demanded it and not because he mourned for her in his heart.

II

THAT silent ghost of a woman being gone, no one could say of him that he was hard; nor could anything be said against him except that he was not a saint, in spite of his name. But, sir, we do not look for saints among strong men, who live in the saddle, and are at the head of big establishments. If there was one who was a father to the poor it was Santos; therefore he was loved by many, and only those who had done him an injury or had crossed him in any way had reason to fear and hate him. But let me now relate what I, a boy of ten, witnessed one day in the year 1808. This will show you what the man's temper was; and his courage, and the strength of his wrists.

It was his custom to pay a visit every two or three months to a monastery at a distance of half-a-day's journey from El Ombú.

He was greatly esteemed by the friars, and whenever he went to see them he had a led horse to carry his presents to the Brothers;—a side of fat beef, a sucking-pig or two, a couple of lambs, when they were in season, a few fat turkeys and ducks, a bunch of big partridges, a brace or two of armadillos, the breast and wings of a fat ostrich; and in summer, a dozen ostriches' eggs, and I know not what besides.

One evening I was at El Ombú, and was just starting for home, when Santos saw me, and cried out, "Get off and let your horse go, Nicandro. I am going to the monastery to-morrow, and you shall ride the laden horse, and save me the trouble of leading it. You will be like a little bird perched on his back and he will not feel your few ounces' weight. You can sleep on a sheepskin in the kitchen, and get up an hour before daybreak."

The stars were still shining when we set out on our journey the next morning, in the month of June, and when we crossed the river Sanborombón at sunrise the earth was all white with hoar frost. At noon, we arrived at our destination, and were received by the friars, who embraced and kissed Santos on both cheeks, and took charge of our horses. After breakfast in the kitchen, the day being now warm and pleasant, we went and sat out of doors to sip maté and smoke, and for an hour or longer, the conversation between Santos and the Brothers had been going on when, all at once, a youth appeared coming at a fast gallop towards the gate, shouting as he came, "Los Ingleses! Los Ingleses!" We all jumped up and ran to the gate, and climbing up by the posts and bars, saw at a distance of less than half-a-league to the east, a great army of men marching in the direction of Buenos Ayres. We could see that the foremost part of the army had come to a halt on the banks of a stream which flows past the monastery and empties itself into the Plata, two leagues further east. The army was all composed of infantry, but a great many persons on horse-back could be seen following it, and these, the young man said, were neighbours who had come out to look at the English invaders; and he also said that the soldiers, on arriving at the stream, had begun to throw away their blankets, and that the people were picking them up. Santos hearing this, said he would go and join the crowd, and mounting his horse and followed by me, and by two of the Brothers, who said they wished to get a few blankets for the monastery, we set out at a gallop for the stream.

Arrived at the spot, we found that the English, not satisfied with the ford, which had a very muddy bottom, had made a new crossing-place for themselves by cutting down the bank on both sides, and that numbers of blankets had been folded and laid in the bed of the stream where it was about twenty-five yards wide. Hundreds of blankets were also being thrown away, and the people were picking them up and loading their horses with them. Santos at once threw himself into the crowd and gathered about a dozen blankets, the best he could find, for the friars; then he gathered a few for himself and ordered me to fasten them on the back of my horse.

The soldiers, seeing us scrambling for the blankets, were much amused; but when one man among us cried out, "These people must be mad to throw their blankets away in cold weather—perhaps their red jackets will keep them warm when they lie down to-night"—there was one soldier who understood, and could speak Spanish, and he replied, "No, sirs, we have no further need of blankets. When we next sleep it will be in the best beds in the capitol." Then Santos shouted back, "That, sirs, will perhaps be a sleep from which some of you will never awake." That speech attracted their attention to Santos, and the soldier who had spoken before returned, "There are not many men like you in these parts, therefore what you say does not alarm us." Then they looked at the friars fastening the blankets Santos had given them on to their horses, and seeing that they wore heavy iron spurs strapped on their bare feet, they shouted with laughter, and the one who talked with us cried out, "We are sorry, good Brothers, that we have not boots as well as blankets to give you."

But our business was now done, and bidding good-bye to the friars, we set out on our return journey, Santos saying that we should be at home before midnight.

It was past the middle of the afternoon, we having ridden about six leagues, when we spied at a distance ahead a great number of mounted men scattered about over the plain, some standing still, others galloping this way or that.

"El pato! el pato!" cried Santos with excitement, "Come, boys, let us go and watch the battle while it is near, and when it is passed on we will go our way." Urging his horse to a gallop, I following, we came to where the men were struggling for the ball, and stood for a while looking on. But it was not in him

to remain a mere spectator for long; never did
he see a cattle-marking, or parting, or races,
or a dance, or any game, and above all games,
el Pato, but he must have a part in it.   Very
soon he dismounted to throw off some of the
heaviest parts of his horse-gear, and ordering
me to take them up on my horse and follow
him, he rode in among the players.

About forty or fifty men had gathered at
that spot, and were sitting quietly on their
horses in a wide circle, waiting to see the result
of a struggle for the Pato between three men
who had hold of the ball.   They were strong
men, well mounted, each resolved to carry off
the prize from the others.   Sir, when I think
of that sight, and remember that the game is
no longer played because of the Tyrant who
forbade it, I am ready to cry out that there
are no longer men on these plains where I first
saw the light!   How they tugged and strained
and sweated, almost dragging each other out
of the saddle, their trained horses leaning
away, digging their hoofs into the turf, as
when they resist the shock of a lassoed animal,
when the lasso stiffens and the pull comes!
One of the men was a big, powerful mulatto,
and the by-standers thinking the victory would

be his, were only waiting to see him wrest the ball from the others to rush upon and try to deprive him of it before he could escape from the crowd.

Santos refused to stand inactive, for was there not a fourth handle to the ball to be grasped by another fighter? Spurring his horse into the group, he very soon succeeded in getting hold of the disengaged handle. A cry of resentment at this action on the part of a stranger went up from some of those who were looking on, mixed with applause at his daring from others, while the three men who had been fighting against each other, each one for himself, now perceived that they had a common enemy. Excited as they were by the struggle, they could not but be startled at the stranger's appearance—that huge man on a big horse, so white-skinned and long-haired, with a black beard, that came down over his breast, and who showed them, when he threw back his poncho, the knife that was like a sword and the big brass-barrelled pistol worn at his waist. Very soon after he joined in the fray all four men came to the earth. But they did not fall together, and the last to go down was Santos, who would not be dragged off his horse, and in the end horse and man came down on the top of the others. In coming down, two of the men had lost their hold of the ball; last of all, the big mulatto, to save himself from being crushed under the falling horse, was forced to let go, and in his rage at being beaten, he whipped out his long knife against the stranger. Santos, too quick for him, dealt him a blow on the forehead with the heavy silver handle of his whip, dropping him stunned to the ground. Of the four, Santos alone had so far escaped injury, and rising and remounting, the ball still in his hand, he rode out from among them, the crowd opening on each side to make room for him.

Now in the crowd there was one tall, imposing-looking man, wearing a white poncho, many silver ornaments, and a long knife in an embossed silver sheath; his horse, too, which was white as milk, was covered with silver trappings. This man alone raised his voice; "Friends and comrades," he cried, "is this to be the finish? If this stranger is permitted to carry the Pato away, it will not be because of his stronger wrist and better horse, but because he carries firearms. Comrades, what do you say?"

But there was no answer. They had seen the power and resolution of the man, and though they were many they preferred to let him go in peace. Then the man on a white horse, with a scowl of anger and contempt, turned from them and began following us at a distance of about fifty yards. Whenever Santos turned back to come to close quarters with him, he retired, only to turn and follow us again as soon as Santos resumed his course. In this way we rode till sunset. Santos was grave, but calm; I, being so young, was in constant terror. "Oh, uncle," I whispered, "for the love of God fire your pistol at this man and kill him, so that he may not kill us!"

Santos laughed. "Fool of a boy," he replied, "do you not know that he wants me to fire at him! He knows that I could not hit him at this distance, and that after discharging my pistol we should be equal, man to man, and knife to knife; and who knows then which would kill the other? God knows best, since He knows everything, and He has put it into my heart not to fire."

When it grew dark we rode slower, and the man then lessened the distance between us. We could hear the chink-chink of his silver trappings, and when I looked back I could see a white misty form following us like a ghost. Then, all at once, there came a noise of hoofs and a whistling sound of something thrown, and Santos' horse plunged and reared and kicked, then stood still trembling with terror. His hind legs were entangled in the bolas which had been thrown. With a curse Santos threw himself off, and, drawing his knife, cut the thong which bound the animal's legs, and remounting we went on as before, the white figure still following us.

At length, about midnight, the Sanborombón was reached, at the ford where we had crossed in the morning, where it was about forty yards wide, and the water only high as the surcingle in the deepest parts.

"Let your heart be glad, Nicandro!" said Santos, as we went down into the water; "for our time is come now, and be careful to do as I bid you."

We crossed slowly, and coming out on the south side, Santos quietly dropped off his horse, and, speaking in a low voice, ordered me to ride slowly on with the two horses and wait for him in the road. He said that the man who followed would not see him crouching under the bank, and thinking it safe would cross over, only to receive the charge fired at a few yards' distance.

That was an anxious interval that followed, I waiting alone, scarcely daring to breathe, staring into the darkness in fear of that white figure that was like a ghost, listening for the pistol shot. My prayer to heaven was to direct the bullet in its course, so that it might go to that terrible man's heart, and we be delivered from him. But there was no shot, and no sound except a faint chink of silver and sound of hoof-beats that came to my ears after a time, and soon ceased to be heard. The man, perhaps, had some suspicion of the other's plan and had given up the chase and gone away.

Nothing more do I remember of that journey which ended at El Ombú at cock-crow, except that at one spot Santos fastened a thong round my waist and bound me before and behind to the saddle to prevent my falling from my horse every time I went to sleep.

III

REMEMBER, Señor, that I have spoken of things that passed when I was small. The memories of that time are few and scattered, like the fragments of tiles and bricks and rusty iron which one may find half-buried among the weeds, where the house once stood. Fragments that once formed part of the building. Certain events, some faces, and some voices, I remember, but I cannot say the year. Nor can I say how many years had gone by after Doña Mericie's death, and after my journey to the monastery. Perhaps they were few, perhaps many. Invasions had come, wars with a foreigner and with the savage, and Independence, and many things had happened at a distance. He, Santos, Ugarte, was older, I know, greyer, when that great misfortune and calamity came to one whom God had created so strong, so brave, so noble. And all on account of a slave, a youth born at El Ombú, who had been preferred above the others by his master. For, as it is said, we breed crows to pick our eyes out. But I will say nothing against that poor youth, who was the cause of the disaster, for it was not wholly his fault. Part of the fault was in Santos—his indomitable temper and his violence. And perhaps, too, the time was come when He who rules over all men had said, "You have raised your voice and have ridden over others long enough. Look, Santos! I shall set My foot upon you, and under it you shall be like a wild pumpkin at the end of summer, when it is dryer and more brittle than an empty egg-shell."

Remember that there were slaves in those days, also that there was a law fixing every man's price, old or young, so that if any slave went, money in hand, to his master and offered him the price of his liberty, from that moment he became a free man. It mattered not that his master wished not to sell him. So just was the law.

Of his slaves Santos was accustomed to say, "These are my children, and serve because they love me, not because they are slaves; and if I were to offer his freedom to any one among them, he would refuse to take it." He saw their faces, not their hearts.

His favourite was Meliton, black but well favoured, and though but a youth, he had authority over the others, and dressed well, and rode his master's best horses, and had horses of his own. But it was never said of him that he gained that eminence by means of flattery and a tongue cunning to frame lies. On the contrary, he was loved by all, even by those he was set above, because of his goodness of heart and a sweet and gay disposition. He was one of those who can do almost anything better than others; whatever his master wanted done, whether it was to ride a race, or break a horse, or throw a lasso, or make a bridle, or whip, or surcingle, or play on a guitar, or sing, or dance, it was Meliton, Meliton. There was no one like him.

Now this youth cherished a secret ambition in his heart, and saved, and saved his money; and at length one day he came with a handful of silver and gold to Santos, and said, "Master, here is the price of my freedom, take it and count it, and see that it is right, and let me remain at El Ombú to serve you henceforth without payment. But I shall no longer be a slave."

Santos took the money into his hand, and

spoke, "It was for this then that you saved, even the money I gave you to spend and to run with, and the money you made by selling the animals I gave you—you saved it for this! Ingrate, with a heart blacker than your skin! Take back the money, and go from my presence, and never cross my path again if you wish for a long life." And with that he hurled the handful of silver and gold into the young man's face with such force, that he was cut and bruised with the coins and well nigh stunned. He went back staggering to his horse, and mounting, rode away, sobbing like a child, the blood running down from his face.

He soon left this neighbourhood and went to live at Las Vivoras, on the Vecino river, south of Dolores, and there made good use of his freedom, buying fat animals for the market; and for a space of two years he prospered, and every man, rich or poor, was his friend. Nevertheless, he was not happy, for his heart was loyal and he loved his old master, who had been a father to him, and desired above all things to be forgiven. And, at length, hoping that Santos had outlived his resentment and would be pleased to see him again, he one day came to El Ombú and asked to see the master.

The old man came out of the house and greeted him jovially. "Ha, Meliton," he cried with a laugh, "you have returned in spite of my warning.   Come down from your horse and let me take your hand once more."

The other, glad to think he was forgiven, alighted, and advancing, put out his hand. Santos took it in his, only to crush it with so powerful a grip, that the young man cried out aloud, and blinded with tears of pain, he did not see that his master had the big brass pistol in his left hand, and did not know that his last moment had come.   He fell with a bullet in his heart.

Look, señor, where I am pointing, twenty yards or so from the edge of the shadow of the ombú, do you see a dark green weed with a yellow flower on a tall stem growing on the short, dry grass?   It was just there, on the very spot where the yellow flower is, that poor Meliton fell, and was left lying, covered with blood, until noon the next day.   For no person dared take up the corpse until the Alcalde had been informed of the matter and had come to inquire into it.

Santos had mounted his horse and gone away without a word, taking the road to Buenos Ayres. He had done that for which he would have to pay dearly; for a life is a life, whether the skin be black or white, and no man can slay another deliberately, in cold blood, and escape the penalty. The law is no respecter of persons, and when he, who commits such a deed, is a man of substance, he must expect that Advocates and Judges, with all those who take up his cause, will bleed him well before they procure him a pardon.

Ugarte cared nothing for that, he had been as good as his word, and the devil in his heart was satisfied. Only he would not wait at his estancia to be taken, nor would he go and give himself up to the authorities, who would then have to place him in confinement, and it would be many months before his liberation. That would be like suffocation to him; to such a man a prison is like a tomb. No, he would go to Buenos Ayres and embark for Montevideo, and from that place he would put the matter in motion, and wait there until it was all settled and he was free to return to El Ombú.

Dead Meliton was taken away and buried in

consecrated ground at Chascomus. Rain fell, and washed away the red stains on the ground. In the spring, the swallows returned and built their nests under the eaves; but Ugarte came not back, nor did any certain tidings of him reach us. It was said, I know not whether truly or not, that the Advocate who defended him, and the Judge of First Instance, who had the case before him, had quarrelled about the division of the reward, and both being rich, proud persons, they had allowed themselves to forget the old man waiting there month after month for his pardon, which never came to him.

Better for him if he never heard of the ruin which had fallen on El Ombú during his long exile. There was no one in authority: the slaves, left to themselves, went away, and there was no person to restrain them. As for the cattle and horses, they were blown away like thistle-down, and everyone was free to pasture his herds and flocks on the land.

The house for a time was in charge of some person placed there by the authorities, but little by little it was emptied of its contents; and at last it was abandoned, and for a long time no one could be found to live in it on account of the ghosts.

IV

THERE was living at that time, a few
leagues from El Ombú, one Valerio de
la Cueva, a poor man, whose all consisted of
a small flock of three or four hundred sheep
and a few horses. He had been allowed to
make a small rancho, a mere hut, to shelter
himself and his wife Donata and their one
child, a boy named Bruno; and to pay for the
grass his few sheep consumed he assisted in the
work at the estancia house. This poor man,
hearing of El Ombú, where he could have
house and ground for nothing, offered himself
as occupant, and in time came with wife and
child and his small flock, and all the furniture
he possessed—a bed, two or three chairs, a pot
and kettle, and perhaps a few other things.
Such poverty El Ombú had not known, but
all others had feared to inhabit such a place on
account of its evil name, so that it was left
for Valerio, who was a stranger in the district.

Tell me, señor, have you ever in your life
met with a man, who was perhaps poor, or

even clothed in rags, and who yet when you had looked at and conversed with him, has caused you to say: Here is one who is like no other man in the world? Perhaps on rising and going out, on some clear morning in summer, he looked at the sun when it rose, and perceived an angel sitting in it, and as he gazed, something from that being fell upon and passed into and remained in him. Such a man was Valerio. I have known no other like him.

"Come, friend Nicandro," he would say, "let us sit down in the shade and smoke our cigarettes, and talk of our animals. Here are no politics under this old ombú, no ambitions and intrigues and animosities—no bitterness except in these green leaves. They are our laurels—the leaves of the ombú. Happy Nicandro, who never knew the life of cities! I wish that I, too, had seen the light on these quiet plains, under a thatched roof. Once I wore fine clothes and gold ornaments, and lived in a great house where there were many servants to wait on me. But happy I have never been. Every flower I plucked changed into a nettle to sting my hand. Perhaps that maleficent one, who has pursued me all my days, seeing me now so humbled and one with the poor, has left me and gone away. Yes, I am poor, and this frayed garment that covers me will I press to my lips because it does not shine with silk and gold embroidery. And this poverty which I have found will I cherish, and bequeath it as a precious thing to my child when I die. For with it is peace."

The peace did not last long; for when misfortune has singled out a man for its prey, it will follow him to the end, and he shall not escape from it though he mount up to the clouds like the falcon, or thrust himself deep down into the earth like the armadillo.

Valerio had been two years at El Ombú when there came an Indian invasion on the southern frontier. There was no force to oppose it; the two hundred men stationed at the Guardia del Azul had been besieged by a part of the invaders in the fort, while the larger number of the savages were sweeping away the cattle and horses from the country all round. An urgent order came to the commander at Chascomus to send a contingent of forty men from the department; and I, then a young man of twenty, who had seen no service, was cited to appear at the Commandancia,

in readiness to march. There I found that
Valerio had also been cited, and from that
moment we were together. Two days later
we were at the Azul, the Indians having retired with their booty; and when all the contingents from the various departments had
come in, the commander, one Colonel Barboza, set out with about six hundred men in
pursuit.

It was known that in their retreat the Indians had broken up their force into several
parties, and that these had taken different
directions, and it was thought that these bodies
would reunite after a time, and that the larger number would return to their territory by
way of Trinqué Lauquén, about seventy-five
leagues west of Azul. Our Colonel's plan
was to go quickly to this point and wait the
arrival of the Indians. It was impossible that
they, burdened with the thousands of cattle
they had collected, could move fast, while we
were burdened with nothing, the only animals
we drove before us being our horses. These
numbered about five thousand, but many were
unbroken mares, to be used as food. Nothing
but mare's flesh did we have to eat.

It was the depth of winter, and worse

weather I have never known. In this desert
I first beheld that whiteness called snow, when
the rain flies like cotton-down before the wind,
filling the air and whitening the whole earth.
All day and every day our clothes were wet,
and there was no shelter from the wind and
rain at night, nor could we make fires with the
soaked grass and reeds, and wood there was
none, so that we were compelled to eat our
mare's flesh uncooked.

Three weeks were passed in this misery,
waiting for the Indians and seeking for them,
with the hills of Gaumini now before us in the
south, and now on our left hand; and still no
sight and no sign of the enemy. It seemed as
if the earth had opened and swallowed him
up. Our Colonel was in despair, and we now
began to hope that he would lead us back to
the Azul.

In these circumstances one of the men, who
was thinly clad and had been suffering from a
cough, dropped from his horse, and it was then
seen that he was likely to die, and that in any
case he would have to be left behind. Finding that there was no hope for him, he begged
that those who were with him would remember, when they were at home again, that he

had perished in the desert and that his soul was suffering in purgatory, and that they would give something to the priests to procure him ease. When asked by his officer to say who his relations were and where they lived, he replied that he had no one belonging to him. He said that he had spent many years in captivity among the Indians at the Salinas Grandes, and that on his return he had failed to find any one of his relations living in the district where he had been born. In answer to further questions, he said that he had been carried away when a small boy, that the Indians on that occasion had invaded the Christian country in the depth of winter, and on their retreat, instead of returning to their own homes, they had gone east, toward the sea coast, and had encamped on a plain by a small stream called Curumamuel, at Los Tres Arroyos, where there was firewood and sweet water, and good grass for the cattle, and where they found many Indians, mostly women and children, who had gone thither to await their coming; and at that spot they had remained until the spring.

The poor man died that night, and we gathered stones and piled them on his body so that the foxes and caranchos should not devour him.

At break of day next morning we were on horseback marching at a gallop toward sunrise, for our Colonel had determined to look for the Indians at that distant spot near the sea where they had hidden themselves from their pursuers so many years before. The distance was about seventy leagues, and the journey took us about nine days. And at last, in a deep valley near the sea, the enemy was discovered by our scouts, and we marched by night until we were within less than a league of their encampment, and could see their fires. We rested there for four hours, eating raw flesh and sleeping. Then every man was ordered to mount his best horse, and we were disposed in a half-moon, so that the free horses could easily be driven before us. The Colonel, sitting on his horse, addressed us, "Boys," he said, "you have suffered much, but now the victory is in our hands, and you shall not lose the reward. All the captives you take, and all the thousands of horses and cattle we succeed in recovering, shall be sold by public auction on our return, and the proceeds divided among you."

He then gave the order, and we moved quietly on for a space of half a league, and coming to the edge of the valley saw it all black with cattle before us, and the Indians sleeping in their camp; and just when the sun rose from the sea and God's light came over the earth, with a great shout we charged upon them. In a moment the multitude of cattle, struck with panic, began rushing away, bellowing in all directions, shaking the earth beneath their hoofs. Our troop of horses, urged on by our yells, were soon in the encampment, and the savages, rushing hither and thither, trying to save themselves, were shot and speared and cut down by swords. One desire was in all our hearts, one cry on all lips—kill! kill! kill! Such a slaughter had not been known for a long time, and birds and foxes and armadillos must have grown fat on the flesh of the heathen we left for them. But we killed only the men, and few escaped; the women and children we made captive.

Two days we spent in collecting the scattered cattle and horses, numbering about ten thousand; then with our spoil we set out on our return and arrived at the Azul at the end of August. On the following day the force was broken up into the separate contingents of which it was composed, and each in its turn was sent to the Colonel's house to be paid. The Chascomus contingent was the last to go up, and on presenting ourselves, each man received two months' soldiers' pay, after which Colonel Barboza came out and thanked us for our services, and ordered us to give up our arms at the fort and go back to our district, every man to his own house.

"We have spent some cold nights in the deserts together, neighbour Nicandro," said Valerio, laughing, "but we have fared well— on raw horse flesh; and now to make it better we have received money. Why, look, with all this money I shall be able to buy a pair of new shoes for Bruno. Brave little man! I can see him toddling about among the cardoon thistles, searching for hens' eggs for his mother, and getting his poor little feet full of thorns. If there should be any change left he shall certainly have some sugar-plums."

But the others on coming to the fort began to complain loudly of the treatment they had received, whereupon Valerio, rebuking them, told them to act like men and tell the Colonel that they were not satisfied, or else hold their peace.

"Will you, Valerio, be our spokesman?" they cried, and he, consenting, they all took up their arms again and followed him back to the Colonel's house.

Barboza listened attentively to what was said and replied that our demands were just. The captives and cattle, he said, had been placed in charge of an officer appointed by the authorities and would be sold publicly in a few days. Let them now return to the fort and give up their arms, and leave Valerio with him to assist in drawing up a formal demand for their share of the spoil.

We then retired once more, giving *vivas* to our Colonel. But no sooner had we given up our arms at the fort than we were sharply ordered to saddle our horses and take our departure. I rode out with the others, but seeing that Valerio did not overtake us I went back to look for him.

This was what had happened. Left alone in his enemy's hands, Barboza had his arms taken from him, then ordered his men to carry him out to the patio and flay him alive. The men hesitated to obey so cruel a command,

and this gave Valerio time to speak; "My Colonel," he said, "you put a hard task on these poor men, and my hide when taken will be of no value to you or to them. Bid them lance me or draw a knife across my throat, and I will laud your clemency."

"You shall not lose your hide nor die," returned the Colonel, "for I admire your courage. Take him, boys, and stake him out, and give him two hundred lashes; then throw him into the road so that it may be known that his rebellious conduct has been punished."

This order was obeyed, and out upon the road he was thrown. A compassionate storekeeper belonging to the place saw him lying there insensible, the carrion-hawks attracted by his naked bleeding body hovering about him; and this good man took him and was ministering to him when I found him. He was lying, face down, on a pile of rugs, racked with pains, and all night long his sufferings were terrible; nevertheless, when morning came, he insisted on setting out at once on our journey to Chascomus. When his pain was greatest and caused him to cry out, the cry, when he saw my face, would turn to a laugh. "You are too tender hearted for this world we live in," he would say. "Think nothing of this, Nicandro. I have tasted man's justice and mercy before now. Let us talk of pleasanter things. Do you know that it is the first of September to-day? Spring has come back, though we hardly notice it yet in this cold southern country. It has been winter, winter with us, and no warmth of sun or fire, and no flowers and no birds' song. But our faces are towards the north now; in a few days we shall sit again in the shade of the old ombú, all our toil and suffering over, to listen to the mangangá humming among the leaves and to the call of the yellow bientevéo. And better than all, little Bruno will come to us with his hands full of scarlet verbenas. Perhaps in a few years' time you, too, will be a father, Nicandro, and will know what it is to hear a child's prattle. Come, we have rested long enough, and have many leagues to ride!"

The leagues were sixty by the road, but something was gained by leaving it, and it was easier for Valerio when the horses trod on the turf. To gallop or to trot was impossible, and even walking I had to keep at his side to support him with my arm; for his back was all one ever-bleeding wound, and his hands were powerless, and all his joints swollen and inflamed as a result of his having been stretched out on the stakes. Five days we travelled, and day by day and night by night he grew feebler, but he would not rest; so long as the light lasted he would be on the road; and as we slowly pressed on, I supporting him, he would groan with pain and then laugh and begin to talk of the journey's end and of the joy of seeing wife and child again.

It was afternoon on the fifth day when we arrived. The sight of the ombú which we had had for hours before us, strongly excited him; he begged me, almost with tears, to urge the horses to a gallop, but it would have killed him, and I would not do it.

No person saw our approach, but the door stood open, and when we had walked our horses to within about twenty yards we heard Bruno's voice prattling to his mother. Then suddenly Valerio slipped from the saddle before I could jump down to assist him, and staggered on for a few paces towards the door. Running to his side I heard his cry—"Donata! Bruno! let my eyes see you! one kiss!" Only then his wife heard, and running out to us, saw him sink, and with one last gasp expire in my arms.

Strange and terrible scenes have I witnessed, but never a sadder one than this! Tell me, señor, are these things told in books,—does the world know them?

Valerio was dead. He who was so brave, so generous even in his poverty, of so noble a spirit, yet so gentle; whose words were sweeter than honey to me! Of what his loss was to others—to that poor woman who was the mother of his one child, his little Bruno—I speak not. There are things about which we must be silent, or say only, turning our eyes up, Has He forgotten us! Does He know? But to me the loss was greater than all losses: for he was my friend, the man I loved above all men, who was more to me than any other, even than Santos Ugarte, whose face I should see no more.

For he, too, was dead.

And now I have once more mentioned the name of that man, who was once so great in this district, let me, before proceeding with the history of El Ombú, tell you his end. I heard of it by chance long after he had been placed under the ground.

It was the old man's custom in that house, on the other side of the Rio de la Plata where he was obliged to live, to go down every day to the waterside. Long hours would he spend there, sitting on the rocks, always with his face towards Buenos Ayres. He was waiting, waiting for the pardon which would, perhaps, in God's good time, come to him from that forgetful place. He was thinking of El Ombú; for what was life to him away from it, in that strange country? And that unsatisfied desire, and perhaps remorse, had, they say, made his face terrible to look at, for it was like the face of a dead man who had died with wide-open eyes.

One day some boatmen on the beach noticed that he was seated on the rocks far out and that when the tide rose he made no movement to escape from the water. They saw him sitting waist-deep in the sea, and when they rescued him from his perilous position and brought him to the shore, he stared at them like a great white owl and talked in a strange way.

"It is very cold and very dark," he said, "and I cannot see your faces, but perhaps you know me. I am Santos Ugarte, of El Ombú. I have had a great misfortune, friends. To-day in my anger I killed a poor youth whom I loved like a son—my poor boy Meliton! Why did he despise my warning and put himself in my way! But I will say no more about that. After killing him I rode away with the intention of going to Buenos Ayres, but on the road I repented of my deed and turned back. I said that with my own hands I would take him up and carry him in, and call my neighbours together to watch with me by his poor body. But, Sirs, the night overtook me and the Sanborombón is swollen with rains, as you no doubt know, and in swimming it I lost my horse. I do not know if he was drowned. Let me have a fresh horse, friends, and show me the way to El Ombú, and God will reward you."

In that delusion he remained till the end, a few days later, when he died. May his soul rest in peace!

V

SEÑOR, when I am here and remember these things, I sometimes say to myself: Why, old man, do you come to this tree to sit for an hour in the shade, since there is not on all these plains a sadder or more bitter place? My answer is, To one who has lived long, there is no house and no spot of ground, overgrown with grass and weeds, where a house once stood and where men have lived, that is not equally sad. For this sadness is in us, in a memory of other days which follows us into all places. But for the child there is no past: he is born into the world light hearted like a bird; for him gladness is everywhere.

That is how it was with little Bruno, too young to feel the loss of a father or to remember him long. It was her great love of this child which enabled Donata to live through so terrible a calamity. She never quitted El Ombú. An embargo had been placed on the estancia so that it could not be sold, and she was not disturbed in her possession of the

house.   She now shared it with an old married
couple, who, being poor and having a few
animals, were glad of a place to live in rent
free.   The man, whose name was Pascual,
took care of Donata's flock and the few cows
and horses she owned along with his own.
He was a simple, good-tempered old man,
whose only fault was indolence, and a love of
the bottle, and of play.   But that mattered
little, for when he gambled he invariably lost,
through not being sober, so that when he had
any money it was quickly gone.

Old Pascual first put Bruno on a horse and
taught him to ride after the flock, and to do a
hundred things.   The boy was like his father,
of a beautiful countenance, with black curling
hair, and eyes as lively as a bird's.   It was not
strange that Donata loved him as no mother
ever loved a son, but as he grew up a perpetual
anxiety was in her heart lest he should hear the
story of his father's death and the cause of it.
For she was wise in this; she knew that the
most dangerous of all passions is that of re-
venge, since when it enters into the heart all
others, good or bad, are driven out, and all
ties and interests and all the words that can
be uttered are powerless to restrain a man;

and the end is ruin. Many times she spoke of this to me, begging me with tears never to speak of my dead friend to Bruno, lest he should discover the truth, and that fatal rage should enter into his heart.

It had been Donata's custom, every day since Valerio's death, to take a pitcher of water, fresh from the well, and pour it out on the ground, on the spot where he had sunk down and expired, without that sight of wife and child, that one kiss, for which he had cried. Who can say what caused her to do such a thing? A great grief is like a delirium, and sometimes gives us strange thoughts, and makes us act like demented persons. It may have been because of the appearance of the dead face as she first saw it, dry and white as ashes, the baked black lips, the look of thirst that would give everything for a drink of cold water; and that which she had done in the days of anguish, of delirium, she had continued to do.

The spot where the water was poured each day being but a few yards from the door of the house was of a dryness and hardness of fire-baked bricks, trodden hard by the feet of I know not how many generations of men, and by hoofs of horses ridden every day to the door. But after a long time of watering a little green began to appear in the one spot; and the green was of a creeping plant with small round malva-like leaves, and little white flowers like porcelain shirt buttons. It spread and thickened, and was like a soft green carpet about two yards long placed on that dry ground, and it was of an emerald greenness all the year round, even in the hot weather when the grass was dead and dry and the plains were in colour like a faded yellow rag.

When Bruno was a boy of fourteen I went one day to help him in making a sheepfold, and when our work was finished in the afternoon we went to the house to sip maté. Before going in, on coming to that green patch, Bruno cried out, "Have you ever seen so verdant a spot as this, Nicandro, so soft and cool a spot to lie down on when one is hot and tired?" He then threw himself down full length upon it, and, lying at ease on his back, he looked up at Donata, who came out to us, and spoke laughingly, "Ah, little mother of my soul! A thousand times have I asked you why you poured water every day on this spot and you would not tell me. Now I have found

out. It was all to make me a soft cool spot
to lie on when I come back tired and hot from
work. Look! is it not like a soft bed with a
green and white velvet coverlid; bring water
now, mother mine, and pour it on my hot,
dusty face."

She laughed, too, poor woman, but I could
see the tears in her eyes—the tears which she
was always so careful to hide from him.

All this I remember as if it had happened
yesterday; I can see and hear it all—Donata's
laugh and the tears in her eyes which Bruno
could not see. I remember it so well because
this was almost the last time I saw her before
I was compelled to go away, for my absence
was long. But before I speak of that change
let me tell you of something that happened
about two years before at El Ombú, which
brought a new happiness into that poor
widow's life.

It happened that among those that had no
right to be on the land, but came and settled
there because there was no one to forbid them,
there was a man named Sanchez, who had built
himself a small rancho about half a league
from the old house, and kept a flock of sheep.
He was a widower with one child, a little girl

named Monica. This Sanchez, although poor, was not a good man, and had no tenderness in his heart. He was a gambler, always away from his rancho, leaving the flock to be taken care of by poor little Monica. In winter it was cruel, for then the sheep travel most, and most of all on cold, rough days; and she without a dog to help her, barefooted on the thistle-grown land, often in terror at the sight of cattle, would be compelled to spend the whole day out of doors. More than once on a winter evening in bad weather I have found her trying to drive the sheep home in the face of the rain, crying with misery. It hurt me all the more because she had a pretty face: no person could fail to see its beauty, though she was in rags and her black hair in a tangle, like the mane of a horse that has been feeding among the burrs. At such times I have taken her up on my saddle and driven her flock home for her, and have said to myself: "Poor lamb without a mother, if you were mine I would seat you on the horns of the moon; but, unhappy one! he whom you call father is without compassion."

At length, Sanchez, finding himself without money, just when strangers from all places were coming to Chascomus to witness a great race, and anxious not to lose this chance of large winnings, sold his sheep, having nothing of more value to dispose of. But instead of winning he lost, and then leaving Monica in a neighbour's house he went away, promising to return for her in a few days. But he did not return, and it was believed by everybody that he had abandoned the child.

It was then that Donata offered to take her and be a mother to the orphan, and I can say, señor, that the poor child's own mother, who was dead, could not have treated her more tenderly or loved her more. And the pretty one had now been Donata's little daughter and Bruno's playmate two years when I was called away, and I saw them not again and heard no tidings of them for a space of five years—the five longest years of my life.

VI

I WENT away because men were wanted for the army, and I was taken. I was away, I have said, five years, and the five would have been ten, and the ten twenty, supposing that life had lasted, but for a lance wound in my thigh, which made me a lame man for the rest of my life. That was the reason of my discharge and happy escape from that purgatory. Once back in these plains where I first saw heaven's light, I said in my heart: I can no longer spring light as a bird on to the back of an unbroken animal and laugh at his efforts to shake me off; nor can I throw a lasso on a running horse or bull and digging my heel in the ground, pit my strength against his; nor can I ever be what I have been in any work or game on horseback or on foot; nevertheless, this lameness, and all I have lost through it, is a small price to pay for my deliverance.

But this is not the history of my life; let me remember that I speak only of those who have

lived at El Ombú in my time, in the old house
which no longer exists.

There had been no changes when I returned,
except that those five years had made Bruno
almost a man, and more than ever like his
father, except that he never had that I-know-
not-what something to love in the eyes which
made Valerio different from all men. Donata was the same, but older. Grey hair had
come to her in her affliction; now her hair
which should have been black was all white—
but she was more at peace, for Bruno was good
to her, and as a widow's only son, was exempt
from military service. There was something
else to make her happy. Those two, who were
everything to her, could not grow up under
one roof and not love; now she could look with
confidence to a union between them, and there
would be no separation. But even so, that
old fear she had so often spoken of to me in
former days was never absent from her heart.

Bruno was now away most of the time, work-
ing as a cattle drover, his ambition being, Donata informed me, to make money so as to buy
everything needed for the house.

I had been back, living in that poor rancho,
half a league from El Ombú, where I first saw

the light, for the best part of a year, when Bruno, who had been away with his employer buying cattle in the south, one day appeared at my place. He had not been to El Ombú, and was silent and strange in his manner, and when we were alone together I said to him: "What has happened to you, Bruno, that you have the face of a stranger and speak in an unaccustomed tone to your friend?"

He answered: "Because you, Nicandro, have treated me like a child, concealing from me that which you ought to have told me long ago, instead of leaving me to learn it by accident from a stranger."

"It has come," I said to myself, for I knew what he meant: then I spoke of his mother.

"Ah, yes," he said with bitterness, "I know now why she pours water fresh from the well every day on that spot of ground near the door. Do you, Nicandro, think that water will ever wash away that old stain and memory? A man who is a man, must in such a thing obey, not a mother's wish, nor any woman, but that something which speaks in his heart."

"Let no such thought dwell in you to make you mad," I replied. "Look, Bruno, my friend's son and my friend, leave it to God who is above us, and who considers and remembers all evil deeds that men do, and desires not that anyone should take the sword out of his hand."

"Who is he—this God you talk of?" he answered. "Have you seen or spoken with him that you tell me what his mind is in this matter? I have only this voice to tell me how a man should act in such a case," and he smote his breast; then overcome with a passion of grief he covered his face with his hands and wept.

Vainly I begged him not to lose himself, telling him what the effect of his attempt, whether he succeeded or failed, would be on Donata and on Monica—it would break those poor women's hearts. I spoke, too, of things I had witnessed in my five years' service; the cruel sentences from which there was no appeal, the torments, the horrible deaths so often inflicted. For these evils there was no remedy on earth: and he, a poor, ignorant boy, what would he do but dash himself to pieces against that tower of brass!

He replied that within that brazen tower there was a heart full of blood; and with that he went away, only asking me as a favour not to tell his mother of this visit to me.

Some ten days later she had a message from him, brought from the capital by a traveller going to the south. Bruno sent word that he was going to Las Mulitas, a place fifty leagues west of Buenos Ayres, to work on an estancia there, and would be absent some months.

Why had he gone thither? Because he had heard that General Barboza—for that man was now a General—owned a tract of land at that place, which the Government had given him as a reward for his services on the southern frontier; and that he had recently returned from the northern provinces to Buenos Ayres and was now staying at this estancia at Las Mulitas.

Donata knew nothing of his secret motives, but his absence filled her with anxiety; and when at length she fell ill I resolved to go in search of the poor youth and try to persuade him to return to El Ombú. But at Las Mulitas I heard that he was no longer there. All strangers had been taken for the army in the frontier department, and Bruno, in spite of his passport, had been forced to go.

When I returned to El Ombú with this sad news Donata resolved at once to go to the capital and try to obtain his release. She was

ill, and it was a long journey for her to perform on horseback, but she had friends to go
with and take care of her. In the end she
succeeded in seeing the President, and throwing herself on her knees before him, and with
tears in her eyes, implored him to let her have
her son back.

He listened to her, and gave her a paper to
take to the War Office. There it was found
that Bruno had been sent to El Rosario, and
an order was despatched for his immediate
release. But when the order reached its destination the unhappy boy had deserted.

That was the last that Donata ever heard of
her son. She guessed why he had gone, and
knew as well as if I had told her that he had
found out the secret so long hidden from him.
Still, being his mother, she would not abandon
hope; she struggled to live. Never did I
come into her presence but I saw in her face
a question which she dared not put in words.
If, it said, you have heard, if you know, when
and how his life ended, tell me now before I
go. But it also said, If you know, do not tell
me so that I and Monica may go on hoping
together to the end.

"I know, Nicandro," she would say, "that

if Bruno returns he will not be the same—the
son I have lost.   For in that one thing he is
not like his father.   Could another be like
Valerio?   No misfortune and no injustice
could change that heart, or turn his sweetness
sour.   In that freshness and gaiety of temper
he was like a child, and Bruno as a child was
like him.   My son! my son! where are you?
God of my soul, grant that he may yet come to
me, though his life be now darkened with some
terrible passion—though his poor hands be
stained with blood, so that my eyes may see
him again before I go!"

But he came not, and she died without seeing him.

VII

IF Monica, left alone in the house with old Pascual and his wife, had been disposed to listen to those who were attracted by her face she might have found a protector worthy of her. There were men of substance among those who came for her. But it mattered nothing to her whether they had land and cattle or not, or what their appearance was, and how they were dressed. Hers was a faithful heart. And she looked for Bruno's return, not with that poor half-despairing hope which had been Donata's, and had failed to keep her alive, but with a hope that sustained and made her able to support the months and years of waiting. She looked for his coming as the night-watcher for the dawn. On summer afternoons, when the heat of the day was over, she would take her sewing outside the gate and sit there by the hour, where her sight commanded the road to the north. From that side he would certainly come. On dark, rainy nights a lantern would be hung on the

wall lest he, coming at a late hour, should miss
the house in the dark.   Glad, she was not, nor
lively; she was pale and thin, and those dark
eyes that looked too large because of her thin-
ness were the eyes of one who had beheld grief.
But with it all, there was a serenity, an air of
one whose tears, held back, would all be shed
at the proper time, when he returned.   And
he would, perhaps, come to-day, or, if not to-
day, then to-morrow, or perhaps the day after,
as God willed.

Nearly three years had passed by since Donata's death when, one afternoon, I rode to El
Ombú, and on approaching the house spied a
saddled horse, which had got loose, going away
at a trot.   I went after, and caught, and led it
back, and then saw that its owner was a traveller, an old soldier, who with or without the
permission of the people of the house, was
lying down and asleep in the shade of the
ombú.

There had lately been a battle in the northern part of the province, and the defeated
force had broken up, and the men carrying
their arms had scattered themselves all over
the country.   This veteran was one of them.

He did not wake when I led the horse up

and shouted to him. He was a man about fifty to sixty years old, grey-haired, with many scars of sword and lance wounds on his sun-blackened face and hands. His carbine was leaning against the tree a yard or two away, but he had not unbuckled his sword and what now attracted my attention as I sat on my horse regarding him, was the way in which he clutched the hilt and shook the weapon until it rattled in its scabbard. His was an agitated sleep; the sweat stood in big drops on his face, he ground his teeth and moaned, and muttered words which I could not catch.

At length, dismounting, I called to him again, then shouted in his ear, and finally shook him by the shoulder. Then he woke with a start, and struggling up to a sitting position, and staring at me like one demented, he exclaimed, "What has happened?"

When I told him about his horse he was silent, and sitting there with eyes cast down, passed his hand repeatedly across his forehead. Never in any man's face had I seen misery compared to his. "Pardon me, friend," he spoke at last. "My ears were so full of sounds you do not hear that I paid little attention to what you were saying."

"Perhaps the great heat of the day has overcome you," I said; "or maybe you are suffering from some malady caused by an old wound
received in fight."

"Yes, an incurable malady," he returned,
gloomily. "Have you, friend, been in the
army?"

"Five years had I served when a wound
which made me lame for life delivered me
from that hell."

"I have served thirty," he returned, "perhaps more. I know that I was very young
when I was taken, and I remember that a woman I called mother wept to see me go. That
any eyes should have shed tears for me! Shall
I now in that place in the South where I was
born find one who remembers my name? I
look not for it! I have no one but this"—and
here he touched his sword.

After an interval, he continued, "We say,
friend, that in the army we can do no wrong,
since all responsibility rests with those who are
over us; that our most cruel and sanguinary
deeds are no more a sin or crime than is the
shedding of the blood of cattle, or of Indians
who are not Christians, and are therefore of
no more account than cattle in God's sight.

We say, too, that once we have become accustomed to kill, not men only, but even those who are powerless to defend themselves—the weak and the innocent—we think nothing of it, and have no compunction nor remorse. If this be so, why does He, the One who is above, torment me before my time? Is it just? Listen: no sooner do I close my eyes than sleep brings to me that most terrible experience a man can have—to be in the midst of a conflict and powerless. The bugles call: there is a movement everywhere of masses of men, foot and horse, and every face has on it the look of one who is doomed. There is a murmur of talking all round me, the officers are shouting and waving their swords; I strive in vain to catch the word of command; I do not know what is happening; it is all confusion, a gloom of smoke and dust, a roar of guns, a great noise and shouting of the enemy charging through us. And I am helpless. I awake, and slowly the noise and terrible scene fade from my mind, only to return when sleep again overcomes me. What repose, what refreshment can I know! Sleep, they say, is a friend to everyone, and makes all equal, the rich and the poor, the guilty and the innocent; they say, too, that this forgetfulness is like a draught of cold water to the thirsty man. But what shall I say of sleep? Often with this blade would I have delivered myself from its torture but for the fear that there may be after death something even worse than this dream."

After an interval of silence, seeing that he had recovered from his agitation, I invited him to go with me to the house. "I see smoke issuing from the kitchen," I said, "let us go in so that you may refresh yourself with maté before resuming your journey."

We went in and found the old people boiling the kettle; and in a little while Monica came in and sat with us. Never did she greet me without that light which was like sunshine in her dark eyes; words were not needed to tell me of the gratitude and friendliness she felt toward me, for she was not one to forget the past. I remember that she looked well that day in her white dress with a red flower. Had not Bruno said that he liked to see her in white, and that a flower on her bosom or in her hair was an ornament that gave her most grace? And Bruno might arrive at any moment. But the sight of that grey-haired veteran in his soiled and frayed uniform, and with his clanking sword and his dark scarred face, greatly disturbed her. I noticed that she grew paler and could scarcely keep her eyes off his face while he talked.

When sipping his maté he told us of fights he had been in, of long marches and sufferings in desert places, and of some of the former men he had served under. Among them he, by chance, named General Barboza.

Monica, I knew, had never heard of that man, and on this account I feared not to speak of him. It had, I said, been reported, I knew not whether truthfully or not, that Barboza was dead.

"On that point I can satisfy you," he returned, "since I was serving with him, when his life came to an end in the province of San Luis about two years ago. He was at the head of nineteen hundred men when it happened, and the whole force was filled with amazement at the event. Not that they regretted his loss; on the contrary, his own followers feared, and were glad to be delivered from him. He exceeded most commanders in ferocity, and was accustomed to say scoffingly to his prisoners that he would not have gunpowder wasted on them. That was not a thing to complain of,

but he was capable of treating his own men as
he treated a spy or a prisoner of war. Many
a one have I seen put to death with a blunted
knife, he, Barboza, looking on, smoking a
cigarette. It was the manner of his death that
startled us, for never had man been seen to
perish in such a way.

"It happened on this march, about a month
before the end, that a soldier named Bracamonte went one day at noon to deliver a letter
from his captain to the General. Barboza
was sitting in his shirt sleeves in his tent when
the letter was handed to him, but just when he
put out his hand to take it the man made an
attempt to stab him. The General throwing
himself back escaped the blow, then instantly
sprang like a tiger upon his assailant, and
seizing him by the wrist, wrenched the weapon
out of his hand only to strike it quick as lightning into the poor fool's throat. No sooner
was he down than the General bending over
him, before drawing out the weapon, called
to those who had run to his assistance to get
him a tumbler. When, tumbler in hand, he
lifted himself up and looked upon them, they
say that his face was of the whiteness of iron
made white in the furnace, and that his eyes

were like two flames. He was mad with
rage, and cried out with a loud voice, "Thus,
in the presence of the army do I serve the
wretch who thought to shed my blood!"
Then with a furious gesture he threw down
and shattered the reddened glass, and bade
them take the dead man outside the camp and
leave him stripped to the vultures.

"This ended the episode, but from that day
it was noticed by those about him that a change
had come over the General. If, friend, you
have served with, or have even seen him, you
know the man he was—tall and well-formed,
blue eyed and fair, like an Englishman, en-
dowed with a strength, endurance and resolution that was a wonder to every one: he was
like an eagle among birds,—that great bird
that has no weakness and no mercy, whose cry
fills all creatures with dismay, whose pleasure
it is to tear his victim's flesh with his crooked
talons. But now some secret malady had
fallen on him which took away all his mighty
strength; the colour of his face changed to
sickly paleness, and he bent forward and
swayed this way and that in the saddle as he
rode like a drunken man, and this strange
weakness increased day by day. It was said

in the army that the blood of the man he had killed had poisoned him. The doctors who accompanied us in this march could not cure him, and their failure so angered him against them that they began to fear for their own safety. They now said that he could not be properly treated in camp, but must withdraw to some town where a different system could be followed; but this he refused to do.

"Now it happened that we had an old soldier with us who was a curandero. He was a native of Santa Fé, and was famed for his cures in his own department; but having had the misfortune to kill a man, he was arrested and condemned to serve ten years in the army. This person now informed some of the officers that he would undertake to cure the General, and Barboza, hearing of it, sent for and questioned him. The curandero informed him that his malady was one which the doctors could not cure. It was a failure of a natural heat of the blood, and only by means of animal heat, not by drugs, could health be recovered. In such a grave case the usual remedy of putting the feet and legs in the body of some living animal opened for the purpose would not be sufficient. Some very large beast should be procured and the patient placed bodily in it.

"The General agreed to submit himself to this treatment; the doctors dared not interfere, and men were sent out in quest of a large animal. We were then encamped on a wide sandy plain in San Luis, and as we were without tents we were suffering much from the great heat and the dust-laden winds. But at this spot the General had grown worse, so that he could no longer sit on his horse, and here we had to wait for his improvement.

"In due time a very big bull was brought in and fastened to a stake in the middle of the camp. A space, fifty or sixty yards round, was marked out and roped round, and ponchos hung on the rope to form a curtain so that what was being done should not be witnessed by the army. But a great curiosity and anxiety took possession of the entire force, and when the bull was thrown down and his agonizing bellowings were heard, from all sides officers and men began to move toward that fatal spot. It had been noised about that the cure would be almost instantaneous, and many were prepared to greet the reappearance of the General with a loud cheer.

"Then very suddenly, almost before the bellowings had ceased, shrieks were heard from
the enclosure, and in a moment, while we all
stood staring and wondering, out rushed the
General, stark naked, reddened with that bath
of warm blood he had been in, a sword which
he had hastily snatched up in his hand.   Leaping over the barrier, he stood still for an instant, then catching sight of the great mass of
men before him he flew at them, yelling and
whirling his sword round so that it looked like
a shining wheel in the sun.   The men seeing
that he was raving mad fled before him, and
for a space of a hundred yards or more he
pursued them; then that superhuman energy
was ended; the sword flew from his hand, he
staggered, and fell prostrate on the earth.
For some minutes no one ventured to approach
him, but he never stirred, and at length, when
examined, was found to be dead."

The soldier had finished his story, and
though I had many questions to ask I asked
none, for I saw Monica's distress, and that she
had gone white even to the lips at the terrible
things the man had related.   But now he had
ended, and would soon depart, for the sun was
getting low.

He rolled up and lighted a cigarette, and was about to rise from the bench, when he said, "One thing I forgot to mention about the soldier Bracamonte, who attempted to assassinate the General. After he had been carried out and stripped for the vultures, a paper was found sewn up in the lining of his tunic, which proved to be his passport, for it contained his right description. It said that he was a native of this department of Chascomus, so that you may have heard of him. His name was Bruno de la Cueva."

Would that he had not spoken those last words! Never, though I live to be a hundred, shall I forget that terrible scream that came from Monica's lips before she fell senseless to the floor!

As I raised her in my arms, the soldier turned and said, "She is subject to fits?"

"No," I replied, "that Bruno, of whose death we have now heard for the first time, was of this house."

"It was destiny that led me to this place," he said, "or perhaps that God who is ever against me; but you, friend, are my witness that I crossed not this threshold with a drawn weapon in my hand." And with these words he took his departure, and from that day to this I have never again beheld his face.

She opened her eyes at last, but the wings of my heart drooped when I saw them, since it was easy to see that she had lost her reason; but whether that calamity or the grief she would have known is greatest who can say? Some have died of pure grief—did it not kill Donata in the end?—but the crazed may live many years. We sometimes think it would be better if they were dead; but not in all cases —not, señor, in this.

She lived on here with the old people, for from the first she was quiet and docile as a child. Finally an order came from a person in authority at Chascomus for those who were in the house to quit it. It was going to be pulled down for the sake of the material which was required for a building in the village. Pascual died about that time, and the widow, now old and infirm, went to live with some poor relations at Chascomus and took Monica with her. When the old woman died Monica remained with these people: she lives with them to this day. But she is free to come and go at will, and is known to all in the village as *la loca del Ombú*. They are kind to her, for her story is known to them, and God has put compassion in their hearts.

To see her you would hardly believe that she is the Monica I have told you of, whom I knew as a little one, running bare-footed after her father's flock. For she has grey hairs and wrinkles now. As you ride to Chascomus from this point you will see, on approaching the lake, a very high bank on your left hand, covered with a growth of tall fennel, hoarhound, and cardoon thistle. There on most days you will find her, sitting on the bank in the shade of the tall fennel bushes, looking across the water. She watches for the flamingoes. There are many of those great birds on the lake, and they go in flocks, and when they rise and travel across the water, flying low, their scarlet wings may be seen at a great distance. And every time she catches sight of a flock moving like a red line across the lake she cries out with delight. That is her one happiness—her life. And she is the last of all those who have lived in my time at El Ombú.

STORY OF A PIEBALD HORSE

STORY OF A PIEBALD HORSE.

THIS is all about a piebald. People there are like birds that come down in flocks, hop about chattering, gobble up their seed, then fly away, forgetting what they have swallowed. I love not to scatter grain for such as these. With you, friend, it is different. Others may laugh if they like at the old man of many stories, who puts all things into his copper memory. I can laugh, too, knowing that all things are ordered by destiny; otherwise I might sit down and cry.

The things I have seen! There was the piebald that died long ago; I could take you to the very spot where his bones used to lie bleaching in the sun. There is a nettle growing on the spot. I saw it yesterday. What important things are these to remember and talk about! Bones of a dead horse and a nettle; a young bird that falls from its nest in the night and is found dead in the morning: puff-balls blown about by the wind: a little lamb left behind by the flock bleating at night amongst the thorns and thistles, where only the fox or wild dog can hear it! Small matters are these, and our lives, what are they? And the people we have known, the men and women who have spoken to us and touched us with warm hands—the bright eyes and red lips! Can we cast these things like dead leaves on the fire? Can we lie down full of heaviness because of them, and sleep and rise in the morning without them? Ah, friend!

Let us to the story of the piebald. There was a cattle-marking at neighbour Sotelo's estancia, and out of a herd of three thousand herd we had to part all the yearlings to be branded. After that, dinner and a dance. At sunrise we gathered, about thirty of us; all friends and neighbours, to do the work. Only with us came one person nobody knew. He joined us when we were on our way to the cattle; a young man, slender, well-formed, of pleasing countenance and dressed as few could dress in those days. His horse also shone with silver trappings. And what an animal! Many horses have I seen in this life, but never one with such a presence as this young stranger's piebald.

Arrived at the herd, we began to separate the young animals, the men riding in couples through the cattle, so that each calf when singled out could be driven by two horsemen, one on each side, to prevent it from doubling back. I happened to be mounted on a demon with a fiery mouth—there was no making him work, so I had to leave the parters and stand with little to do, watching the yearlings already parted, to keep them from returning to the herd.

Presently neighbour Chapaco rode up to me. He was a good-hearted man, well-spoken, half Indian and half Christian; but he also had another half, and that was devil.

"What! neighbour Lucero, are you riding on a donkey or a goat, that you remain here doing boy's work?"

I began telling him about my horse, but he did not listen; he was looking at the parters.

"Who is that young stranger?" he asked.

"I see him to-day," I replied, "and if I see him again to-morrow then I shall have seen him twice."

"And in what country of which I have never heard did he learn cattle-parting?" said he.

"He rides," I answered, "like one presuming on a good horse. But he is safe, his fellow-worker has all the danger."

"I believe you," said Chapaco. "He charges furiously and hurls the heifer before his comrade, who has all the work to keep it from doubling, and all the danger, for at any moment his horse may go over it and fall. This our young stranger does knowingly, thinking that no one here will resent it. No, Lucero, he is presuming more on his long knife than on his good horse."

Even while we spoke, the two we were watching rode up to us. Chapaco saluted the young man, taking off his hat, and said—"Will you take me for a partner, friend?"

"Yes; why not, friend?" returned the other; and together the two rode back to the herd.

Now I shall watch them, said I to myself, to see what this Indian devil intends doing. Soon they came out of the herd driving a very small animal. Then I knew what was coming. "May your guardian angel be with you to avert a calamity, young stranger!" I exclaimed. Whip and spur those two came towards me like men riding a race and not parting cattle. Chapaco kept close to the calf, so that he had the advantage, for his horse was well trained. At length he got a little ahead, then, quick as lightning, he forced the calf round square before the other. The piebald struck it full in the middle, and fell because it had to fall. But, Saints in Heaven! why did not the rider save himself? Those who were watching saw him throw up his feet to tread his horse's neck and leap away; nevertheless man, horse, and calf came down together. They ploughed the ground for some distance, so great had been their speed, and the man was under. When we picked him up he was senseless, the blood flowing from his mouth. Next morning, when the sun rose and God's light fell on the earth, he expired.

Of course there was no dancing that night. Some of the people, after eating, went away; others remained sitting about all night, talking in low tones, waiting for the end. A few of us were at his bedside watching his white face and closed eyes. He breathed, and that was all. When the sunlight came over the world he opened his eyes, and Sotelo asked him how he did. He took no notice, but presently his lips began to move, though they seemed to utter no sound. Sotelo bent his ear down to

listen. "Where does she live?" he asked.
He could not answer—he was dead.

"He seemed to be saying many things," Sotelo told us, "but I understood only this—
'Tell her to forgive me . . . I was wrong.
She loved him from the first. . . . I was
jealous and hated him. . . . Tell Elaria not
to grieve—Anacleto will be good to her.'
Alas! my friends, where shall I find his relations to deliver this dying message to them?"

The Alcalde came that day and made a list
of the dead man's possessions, and bade Sotelo
take charge of them till the relations could be
found.   Then, calling all the people together,
he bade each person cut on his whip-handle
and on the sheath of his knife the mark branded
on the flank of the piebald, which was in shape
like a horse-shoe with a cross inside, so that it
might be shown to all strangers, and made
known through the country until the dead
man's relations should hear of it.

When a year had gone by, the Alcalde told
Sotelo that, all inquiries having failed, he
could now take the piebald and the silver trappings for himself.   Sotelo would not listen to
this, for he was a devout man and coveted no
person's property, dead or alive.   The horse

and things, however, still remained in his charge.

Three years later I was one afternoon sitting with Sotelo, taking maté, when his herd of dun mares were driven up. They came galloping and neighing to the corral and ahead of them, looking like a wild horse, was the piebald, for no person ever mounted him.

"Never do I look on that horse," I remarked, "without remembering the fatal marking, when its master met his death."

"Now you speak of it," said he, "let me inform you that I am about to try a new plan. That noble piebald and all those silver trappings hanging in my room are always reproaching my conscience. Let us not forget the young stranger we put under ground. I have had many masses said for his soul's repose, but that does not quite satisfy me. Somewhere there is a place where he is not forgotten. Hands there are, perhaps, that gather wild flowers to place them with lighted candles before the image of the Blessed Virgin; eyes there are that weep and watch for his coming. You know how many travellers and cattle-drovers going to Buenos Ayres from the south call for refreshment at the *pulperia*.

I intend taking the piebald and trying him every day at the gate there. No person calling will fail to notice the horse, and some day perhaps some traveller will recognise the brand on its flank and will be able to tell us what department and what estancia it comes from."

I did not believe anything would result from this, but said nothing, not wishing to discourage him.

Next morning the piebald was tied up at the gate of the *pulperia,* at the road side, only to be released again when night came, and this was repeated every day for a long time. So fine an animal did not fail to attract the attention of all strangers passing that way, still several weeks went by and nothing was discovered. At length, one evening, just when the sun was setting, there appeared a troop of cattle driven by eight men. It had come a great distance, for the troop was a large one— about nine hundred head—and they moved slowly, like cattle that had been many days on the road. Some of the men came in for refreshments; then the store-keeper noticed that one remained outside leaning on the gate.

"What is the capatas doing that he remains outside?" said one of the men.

"Evidently he has fallen in love with that piebald," said another, "for he cannot take his eyes off it."

At length the capatas, a young man of good presence, came in and sat down on a bench. The others were talking and laughing about the strange things they had all been doing the day before; for they had been many days and nights on the road, only nodding a little in their saddles, and at length becoming delirious from want of sleep, they had begun to act like men that are half-crazed.

"Enough of the delusions of yesterday," said the capatas, who had been silently listening to them, "but tell me, boys, am I in the same condition to-day?"

"Surely not!" they replied. "Thanks to those horned devils being so tired and foot-sore, we all had some sleep last night."

"Very well then," said he, "now you have finished eating and drinking, go back to the troop, but before you leave look well at that piebald tied at the gate. He that is not a cattle-drover may ask, 'How can my eyes deceive me?' but I know that a crazy brain makes us see many strange things when the drowsy eyes can only be held open with the fingers."

The men did as they were told, and when they had looked well at the piebald, they all shouted out, "He has the brand of the estancia de Silva on his flank, and no counter-brand— claim the horse, capatas, for he is yours." And after that they rode away to the herd.

"My friend," said the capatas to the store-keeper, "will you explain how you came possessed of this piebald horse?"

Then the other told him everything, even the dying words of the young stranger, for he knew all.

The capatas bent down his head, and covering his face shed tears. Then he said, "And you died thus, Torcuato, amongst strangers! From my heart I have forgiven you the wrong you did me. Heaven rest your soul, Torcuato; I cannot forget that we were once brothers. I, friend, am that Anacleto of whom he spoke with his last breath."

Sotelo was then sent for, and when he arrived and the *pulperia* was closed for the night, the capatas told his story, which I will give you in his own words, for I was also present to hear him. This is what he told us:—

I was born on the southern frontier. My parents died when I was very small, but Heaven had compassion on me and raised up one to shelter me in my orphanhood. Don Loreto Silva took me to his estancia on the Sarandi, a stream half a day's journey from Tandil, towards the setting sun. He treated me like one of his own children, and I took the name of Silva. He had two other children, Torcuato, who was about the same age as myself, and his daughter, Elaria, who was younger. He was a widower when he took charge of me, and died when I was still a youth. After his death we moved to Tandil, where we had a house close to the little town; for we were all minors, and the property had been left to be equally divided between us when we should be of age. For four years we lived happily together; then when we were of age we preferred to keep the property undivided. I proposed that we should go and live on the estancia, but Torcuato would not consent, liking the place where we were living best. Finally, not being able to persuade him, I resolved to go and attend to the estancia my-

self.   He said that I could please myself and
that he should stay where he was with Elaria.
It was only when I told Elaria of these things
that I knew how much I loved her.   She wept
and implored me not to leave her.

"Why do you shed tears, Elaria?" I said;
"is it because you love me?   Know, then, that
I also love you with all my heart, and if you
will be mine, nothing can ever make us unhappy.   Do not think that my absence at the
estancia will deprive me of this feeling which
has ever been growing up in me."

"I do love you, Anacleto," she replied, "and
I have also known of your love for a long
time.   But there is something in my heart
which I cannot impart to you; only I ask you,
for the love you bear me, do not leave me, and
do not ask me why I say this to you."

After this appeal I could not leave her, nor
did I ask her to tell me her secret.   Torcuato
and I were friendly, but not as we had been
before this difference.   I had no evil thoughts
of him; I loved him and was with him continually; but from the moment I announced to
him that I had changed my mind about going
to the estancia, and was silent when he de-

manded the reason, there was a something in him which made it different between us. I could not open my heart to him about Elaria, and sometimes I thought that he also had a secret which he had no intention of sharing with me. This coldness did not, however, distress me very much, so great was the happiness I now experienced, knowing that I possessed Elaria's love. He was much away from the house, being fond of amusements, and he had also begun to gamble. About three months passed in this way, when one morning Torcuato, who was saddling his horse to go out, said, "Will you come with me, to-day, Anacleto?"

"I do not care to go," I answered.

"Look, Anacleto," said he; "once you were always ready to accompany me to a race or dance or cattle-marking. Why have you ceased to care for these things? Are you growing devout before your time, or does my company no longer please you?"

"It is best to tell him everything and have done with secrets," said I to myself, and so replied—

"Since you ask me, Torcuato, I will answer

you frankly. It is true that I now take less pleasure than formerly in these pastimes; but you have not guessed the reason rightly."

"What then is this reason of which you speak?"

"Since you cannot guess it," I replied, "know that it is love."

"Love for whom?" he asked quickly, and turning very pale.

"Do you need ask? Elaria," I replied.

I had scarcely uttered the name before he turned on me full of rage.

"Elaria!" he exclaimed. "Do you dare tell me of love for Elaria! But you are only a blind fool, and do not know that I am going to marry her myself."

"Are you mad, Torcuato, to talk of marrying your sister?"

"She is no more my sister than you are my brother," he returned. "I," he continued, striking his breast passionately, "am the only child of my father, Loreto Silva. Elaria, whose mother died in giving her birth, was adopted by my parents. And because she is going to be my wife, I am willing that she should have a share of the property; but you, a miserable foundling, why were you lifted up so high? Was it not enough that you were clothed and fed till you came to man's estate? Not a hand's-breadth of the estancia land should be yours by right, and now you presume to speak of love for Elaria."

My blood was on fire with so many insults, but I remembered all the benefits I had received from his father, and did not raise my hand against him. Without more words he left me. I then hastened to Elaria and told her what had passed.

"This," I said, "is the secret you would not impart to me. Why, when you knew these things, was I kept in ignorance?"

"Have pity on me, Anacleto," she replied, crying. "Did I not see that you two were no longer friends and brothers, and this without knowing of each other's love? I dared not open my lips to you or to him. It is always a woman's part to suffer in silence. God intended us to be poor, Anacleto, for we were both born of poor parents, and had this property never come to us, how happy we might have been!"

"Why do you say such things, Elaria? Since we love each other, we cannot be unhappy, rich or poor."

"Is it a little matter," she replied, "that Torcuato must be our bitter enemy?   But you do not know every thing.   Before Torcuato's father died, he said he wished his son to marry me when we came of age.   When he spoke about it we were sitting together by his bed."

"And what did you say, Elaria?" I asked, full of concern.

"Torcuato promised to marry me.   I only covered my face, and was silent, for I loved you best even then, though I was almost a child, and my heart was filled with grief at his words.   After we came here, Torcuato reminded me of his father's words.   I answered that I did not wish to marry him, that he was only a brother to me.   Then he said that we were young and he could wait until I was of another mind.   This is all I have to say; but how shall we three live together any longer?   I cannot bear to part from you, and every moment I tremble to think what may happen when you two are together."

"Fear   nothing,"   I   said.   "To-morrow morning you can go to spend a week at some friend's house in the town; then I will speak to Torcuato, and tell him that since we cannot live in peace together we must separate.

Even if he answers with insults I shall do nothing to grieve you, and if he refuses to listen to me, I shall send some person we both respect to arrange all things between us."

This satisfied her, but as evening approached she grew paler, and I knew she feared Torcuato's return. He did not, however, come back that night. Early next morning she was ready to leave. It was an easy walk to the town, but the dew was heavy on the grass, and I saddled a horse for her to ride. I had just lifted her to the saddle when Torcuato appeared. He came at great speed, and throwing himself off his horse, advanced to us. Elaria trembled and seemed ready to sink upon the earth to hide herself like a partridge that has seen the hawk. I prepared myself for insults and perhaps violence. He never looked at me; he only spoke to her.

"Elaria," he said, "something has happened —something that obliges me to leave this house and neighbourhood at once. Remember when I am away that my father, who cherished you and enriched you with his bounty, and who also cherished and enriched this ingrate, spoke to us from his dying bed and made me promise to marry you. Think what his love was; do not forget that his last wish is sacred, and that Anacleto has acted a base, treacherous part in trying to steal you from me. He was lifted out of the mire to be my brother and equal in everything except this. He has got a third part of my inheritance—let that satisfy him; your own heart, Elaria, will tell you that a marriage with him would be a crime before God and man. Look not for my return to-morrow nor for many days. But if you two begin to laugh at my father's dying wishes, look for me, for then I shall not delay to come back to you, Elaria, and to you, Anacleto. I have spoken."

He then mounted his horse and rode away. Very soon we learned the cause of his sudden departure. He had quarrelled over his cards and in a struggle that followed had stabbed his adversary to the heart. He had fled to escape the penalty. We did not believe that he would remain long absent; for Torcuato was very young, well off, and much liked, and this was, moreover, his first offence against the law. But time went on and he did not return, nor did any message from him reach us, and we at last concluded that he had left the country. Only now after four years have

I accidentally discovered his fate through seeing his piebald horse.

After he had been absent over a year, I
asked Elaria to become my wife. "We cannot marry till Torcuato returns," she said.
"For if we take the property that ought to
have been all his, and at the same time disobey
his father's dying wish, we shall be doing an
evil thing. Let us take care of the property
till he returns to receive it all back from us;
then, Anacleto, we shall be free to marry."

I consented, for she was more to me than
lands and cattle. I put the estancia in order
and leaving a trustworthy person in charge of
everything I invested my money in fat bul-
locks to resell in Buenos Ayres, and in this
business I have been employed ever since.
From the estancia I have taken nothing, and
now it must all come back to us—his inheritance and ours. This is a bitter thing and
will give Elaria great grief.

Thus ended Anacleto's story, and when he
had finished speaking and still seemed greatly
troubled in his mind, Sotelo said to him,
"Friend, let me advise you what to do. You
will now shortly be married to the woman you

love and probably some day a son will be born to you. Let him be named Torcuato, and let Torcuato's inheritance be kept for him. And if God gives you no son, remember what was done for you and for the girl you are going to marry, when you were orphans and friendless, and look out for some unhappy child in the same condition, to protect and enrich him as you were enriched."

"You have spoken well," said Anacleto. "I will report your words to Elaria, and whatever she wishes done that will I do."

So ends my story, friend. The cattle-drover left us that night and we saw no more of him. Only before going he gave the piebald and the silver trapping to Sotelo. Six months after his visit, Sotelo also received a letter from him to say that his marriage with Elaria had taken place; and the letter was accompanied with a present of seven cream-coloured horses with black manes and hoofs.

PELINO VIERA'S CONFESSION

PELINO VIERA'S CONFESSION

IT will be necessary to inform the reader—
in all probability unacquainted with the
political events of 1829 in Buenos Ayres—that
the close of that year was more memorable for
tumults of a revolutionary character than
usual. During these disturbances the prisoners confined in the city gaol, taking advantage
of the outside agitation and of the weakness
of their guard, made an attempt to recover
their liberty. They were not acting without
precedent, and had things taken their usual
course they would, no doubt, have succeeded
in placing themselves beyond the oppressive
tyranny of the criminal laws. Unfortunately
for them they were discovered in time and
fired on by the guard; several were killed or
wounded, and in the end they were over-
powered; not, however, before some half-
dozen of them had made good their escape.
Amongst the few thus favoured of fortune was
Pelino Viera, a prisoner who had already been
found guilty—without extenuating circum-

stances—of murdering his wife. Notwithstanding the unsettled condition of the country
the tragedy had created a great sensation at
the time, owing to the unusual circumstances
attending it. Viera was a young man of good
standing, and generally liked for the sweetness of his disposition; he had married a very
beautiful woman, and was believed by all who
knew him to entertain the deepest affection
for her. What then was the motive of the
crime? The mystery remained unsolved at
the trial, and the learned and eloquent Doctor
of Laws who defended Viera was evidently
put to great straits, since the theory he set up
was characterised by the Judge of First Instance, presiding at the trial, as incredible and
even absurd. It was to the effect that Viera's
wife was a somnambulist; that roaming about
her bedchamber she had knocked down a
rapier hanging against the wall, which falling
pierced her bosom; and that Viera, distracted
at so sudden and awful a calamity, had been
unable to give an account of what had happened, but had only raved incoherently when
discovered mourning over the corpse of his
bride. The accused himself would not open
his lips either to confess or to deny his guilt,

but appeared, while the trial lasted, like one overwhelmed by a great despair. He was accordingly condemned to be shot; those who saw him carried back to his cell knew there was not the smallest chance of a reprieve, even in a country where reprieves may often be had for the asking: for the unhappy man's relations were thousands of miles away and ignorant of his desperate situation, while his wife's family were only too anxious to see the last penalty of the law inflicted on him. Unexpectedly, when the young wife-killer imagined that only two days of life remained to him, his fellow-prisoners dragged him forth from his cell, and from that moment he vanished utterly from sight. Concealed in the pallet he had occupied the following confession was found, written in pencil on a few sheets of the large Barcelona paper which it is customary to give out to the prisoners to make their cigarettes with. The manuscript was preserved, along with other prison curiosities, by the gaoler, and after his death, many years ago, it came by chance into my possession.

I am not going to shock the enlightened and scientific reader by expressing belief in this confession, but give, without comment, a simple translation of it. Witchcraft in England is dead and buried; and if sometimes it rises out of its grass-grown grave it returns to us under some new and pretty name, and can no longer be recognised as that maleficent something which was wont to trouble the peace of our forefathers. But in Pelino Viera's country it is or still was in his day, a reality and a power. There, at the hour of midnight it is a common thing to be startled by peals of shrill hysterical laughter, heard far up in the sky; this is called the *witch-laughter,* and something about what is supposed to be the cause of it may be gathered from what follows.

My father came early in life to this city as agent for a commercial firm in Lisbon. In time he prospered greatly, and for over twenty years figured as one of the principal merchants of Buenos Ayres. At length he resolved to give up business and spend the remainder of his days in his own country. The very thought of going to Portugal was to me intolerable. By birth and education I was an Argentine, and looked upon the Portuguese as a distant people about whom we knew nothing, except that they were of the same race as the

Brazilians, our natural enemies. My father consented to let me remain; he had nine children and could afford to spare me; nor did my mother regard the separation as a calamity, for I was not her favourite son. Before embarking my father made generous provision for my support. Knowing that my preference was for a country life, he gave me a letter to Don Hilario Roldan, a wealthy landholder of Los Montes Grandes—a pastoral district in the southern portion of the province; and told me to go and reside with Roldan, who would be a second father to me. He also gave me to understand that a sum of money, sufficient for the purchase of an estate, would be lodged for me with his old friend.

After parting from my relations on board their ship I despatched a letter to Don Hilario, informing him of my intended visit, and then spent a few days making preparations for my country life. I sent my luggage on by the diligence, then, having provided myself with a good horse, I left Buenos Ayres, intending to journey leisurely to the Espinillo, Roldan's estate. I rode slowly across country, inquiring my way and resting every night at some village or estancia house. On the afternoon

of the third day I came in sight of the Espinillo—a herdsman pointed it out to me—a blue
line of trees on the distant horizon.   My horse
being tired when I approached my destination,
I walked him slowly through the wood of tala
trees.   Here the boles and lower branches had
been rubbed smooth by the cattle, and there
was no underwood.   Finding the shade grateful and wishing to feel my feet on the ground,
I dismounted and led my horse by the bridle.
A great silence rested on the earth; only the
distant lowing of cattle could be heard, and
sometimes a wild bird broke into song near
me.   This quiet of nature was grateful to me;
I could not have wished for a sweeter welcome.
Suddenly as I walked I heard before me the
shrill voices of women quarrelling: they
seemed to be very angry, and some of the ex-
pressions they used were dreadful to hear.
Very soon I caught sight of them.   One was
a withered, white-haired old woman, dressed
in rags, and holding in her arms a bundle of
dried sticks.   The other was young, and wore
a dark-green dress; her face was white with
passion, and I saw her strike the old woman
a blow that made her stagger and drop her
bundle of sticks on the ground.   At this mo-

ment they perceived me. The young woman
had a grey shawl with a green fringe on her
arm, and on seeing me she wrapped up her
face in it, and hurried away through the trees.
The other, snatching up her bundle, hobbled
off in an opposite direction. When I called
to her she only increased her pace, and I was
left alone. I continued my walk, and presently emerging from the road I found myself
before the house I sought.

Don Hilario had not visited Buenos Ayres
for many years, and I did not remember him.
He was a stout, elderly man, with white hair,
which he wore long, and a pleasing, open,
florid countenance. He embraced me joyfully, asked me a hundred questions, and talked
and laughed incessantly, so pleased was he at
my visit. Later he presented me to his daughters, and I was surprised and flattered at the
warmth of their welcome.

Don Hilario had a gay, lively disposition,
and, remarking my white hands, asked me if
I thought they could check a hot-mouthed
horse, or cast a lasso on to the horns of a bull.
After dinner, when we all sat under the corri-
dor to enjoy the cool evening, I began to ob-
serve his daughters more closely. The young-

est, whose name was Dolores, was a gentle-
faced girl, with grey eyes and chestnut hair.
Apart from her sister she would have been
greatly admired. Her sister, Rosaura, was
one of those women who are instantly pronounced beautiful by all who see them. Her
eyes were dark and passionate, her features
perfect; never had I seen anything to compare
with the richness of her complexion, shaded
by luxuriant masses of blue-black hair. I
tried to restrain the spontaneous admiration I
felt. I desired to look on her with calm indifference, or only with an interest like that felt
for rare and lovely flowers by one learned in
plants. If a thought of love was born in me, I
regarded it as a dangerous thought, and strove
to divest myself of it. Was any defence against
such sweetness possible? She fascinated me.
Every glance, every word, every smile drew
me irresistibly to her. Yet the struggle in me
would not cease. What is the reason of this
unwillingness to submit? I asked myself. The
answer took the form of a painful suspicion. I
remembered that scene in the tala wood, and
imagined that in Rosaura I beheld that angry
young woman of the green dress. In another

moment I rebuked a thought so unjust.   I was
about to relate to her what I had witnessed.
Again and again I attempted to speak of it,
but though rebuked, the suspicion still lived
and made me silent.

For many days these thoughts continued to
disquiet me, and made me anxiously watch for
the appearance of the green dress and of the
shawl with green fringe.   I never saw them.
Days, weeks, months flew pleasantly by; I had
lived an entire year at the Espinillo.   Roldan
treated me like a beloved son.   I acted as
major-domo on the estate, and the free life of
the pampas grew unspeakably dear to me.   I
could understand why those who have once
tasted it are never satisfied with any other.
The artificial luxuries of cities, the excitement
of politics, the delights of travel—what are
these in comparison with it?   The sisters were
my constant companions.   With them I rode,
walked, sang, or conversed at all hours of the
day.   Dolores was my sweet sister, and I was
her brother; but Rosaura—if I but touched
her hand my heart was on fire; I trembled
and could not speak for joy.   And she was not
indifferent to me.   How could I fail to re-

mark the rich colour that mantled her olive
cheek, the fire that flashed from her dark eyes
at my approach?

One evening Roldan hurried in full of
happy excitement. "Pelino!" he cried, "I
bring you great news! The estate adjoining
mine on the west side is for sale—two leagues
of incomparable pasture land. The thing
could not be better. The Verro—a perennial
stream, remember—runs the entire length of
the land. Will you now begin life for yourself? I advise you to buy, build a proper
house, plant trees, and make a paradise. If
your money is not sufficient, let me help you.
I am rich and have few mouths to feed."

I did as he advised. I bought the estate,
built houses, and increased the stock. The
care of my new establishment, which I had re-
christened Santa Rosaura, occupied all my
time, so that my visits to my friends became
infrequent. At first I could scarcely exist
apart from Rosaura; her image was before me
day and night, while the craving to be with
her was so intense that I lost flesh and looked
pale and worn. I was therefore surprised to
find this great longing quickly pass away. My

mind was again serene as in the days before
that great passion had disturbed me. At the
same time, however, I felt that only while
apart from Rosaura would this feeling of freedom which I had now recovered endure, so
that I grew more and more reluctant to visit
her.

I had been about four months at Santa
Rosaura when Roldan came one day to visit
me. After admiring all I had done he asked
me how I bore my solitary life.

"Ah, there it is!" I replied. "I miss your
pleasant society every hour of the day."

The old man's face darkened, for by nature
he was proud and passionate. "And is the society of my daughters nothing to you, Pelino?"
he sternly said.

"What must I say to him now?" I asked myself, and was silent.

"Pelino," he demanded, "have you nothing
to answer? I have been a father to you. I
am an old and wealthy man; remember that
I am also a proud one. Have I not seen everything since the day that brought you to my
door? You have won the heart of the
daughter I idolise. I never spoke a word to

you, remembering whose son you were, and
that a Viera should be incapable of a dishon-
ourable action."

The old man's just anger and my facile nature conspired to destroy me. "Oh, señor," I
exclaimed, "I should indeed be the basest of
men had any motive but the purest love and es-
teem influenced me. To possess your daughter's affections would indeed be the greatest
happiness. I have loved and I love her. But
has she given me her heart? On that point
I have only cruel doubts."

"And are you so weak as to resign your hopes
because of doubts?" asked Roldan with a touch
of scorn. "Speak to her, boy, and you will
know all. And should she refuse you, swear
by all you hold sacred to marry her in spite
of refusals. That was what I did, Pelino, and
the woman I won—Heaven rest her soul!—
was like her daughter Rosaura."

I clasped his hand and thanked him for
the encouragement he gave me. The cloud
passed from his brow, and we parted friends.

Notwithstanding all I had said I was filled
with despondency when he left me. True, I
loved Rosaura, but the thought of an alliance
with her was almost intolerable. Yet what

could I do? From the alternative course I shrank in dismay, for how could I ever endure to be despised by Roldan, whom I loved, as the vilest of men? I saw no possible escape from the false position I was in. My mind was in a dreadful tumult, and in this condition I passed several days and nights. I tried to force myself to believe that I loved Rosaura passionately, as I had indeed loved her once, and that were I to marry her, a great and enduring happiness would crown my life. I figured her in my mind a bride, dwelling in imagination on her perennial smile, her passionate beauty, her thousand nameless fascinations. All in vain! Only the image of the white-faced fury of the tala wood remained persistently on my mind, and my heart sank within me. At length, driven to extremity, I resolved to prove the truth of my suspicions. Never would such a fiend win me to marry her, though her beauty exceeded that of an angel! Suddenly a means of escape opened before me. I will visit Rosaura, I said, and tell her of that strange scene in the tala wood. Her confusion will betray her. I will be grieved, alarmed, amazed. I will discover by accident, as it were, in her that hateful being. Then I will

not spare her, but wound her with cruel taunts;
her agitation will turn to implacable rage, and
our miserable affair will end in mutual insults. Roldan, ignorant of the cause of our
quarrel, will be unable to blame me. Having
thus carefully considered my plans and prepared myself for the exercise of dissimulation,
I went to the Espinillo.

Roldan was absent. Dolores received me;
her sister, she told me, was far from well, and
for some days past had kept her room. I expressed sympathy and sent a kind message. I
was left alone for half an hour, and experienced the greatest agitation of mind. I was
now, perhaps, about to be subjected to a terrible trial, but the happiness of my whole life
depended on my resolution, and I was determined to allow no soft feelings to influence me.

At length Dolores returned supporting her
sister, who advanced with feeble steps to meet
me. What a change in her face—how thin
and pale it was! Yet never had I seen her
fairer: the pensive languor of illness, her
pallor, the eyes cast down, and the shy fond-
ness with which she regarded me, increased her
beauty a thousand times. I hastened to her
side and clasped her hand in mine, and could

not withdraw my sight from her countenance. For a few moments she permitted me to retain her hand, then gently withdrew it. Her eyes drooped and her face became suffused with a soft indescribable loveliness. When Dolores left us I could no longer disguise my feelings, and tenderly upbraided her for having kept me in ignorance of her illness. She turned her face aside and burst into a flood of tears. I implored her to tell me the secret of her grief.

"If this is grief, Pelino," she replied, "then it is indeed sweet to grieve. Oh, you do not know how dear you are to us all in this house. What would our lonely lives be without your friendship? And you grew so cold towards us I thought it was about to end for ever. I knew, Pelino, I had never uttered a word, never harboured a thought you could take offence at, and feared that some cruel falsehood had come between us. Will you now always —always be our friend, Pelino?"

I replied by clasping her to my bosom, pressing a hundred burning kisses on her sweet lips, and pouring a thousand tender vows of eternal love in her ear. What supreme happiness I felt! I now looked back on my former state as madness. For what insane delusions, what lies whispered by some malignant fiend, had made me harbour cruel thoughts of this precious woman I loved, this sweetest creature Heaven had made? Never, so long as life lasted, should anything come between us again!

Not very long after that meeting we were married. For three happy months we resided in Buenos Ayres, visiting my wife's relations. Then we returned to Santa Rosaura, and I was once more occupied with my flocks and herds and the pastimes of the pampas.

Life was now doubly sweet for the presence of the woman I idolised. Never had man a more beautiful or a more devoted wife, and the readiness, nay joy, with which she resigned the luxuries and gay pastimes of the capital to accompany me to our home in the lonely pampa filled me with a pleasant surprise. Still even then my mind had not regained its calm; the delirious happiness I experienced was not a dress for everyday wear, but a gay, embroidered garment that would soon lose its gloss.

Eight months had elapsed since my return, when, turning my eyes inward and considering my state, as those who have been disturbed in their minds are accustomed to do, I made the discovery that I was no longer happy. "Ingrate, fool, dreamer of vain dreams, what would you have?" I said to myself, striving to overcome the secret melancholy corroding my heart. Had I ceased to love my wife? She was still all my imagination had pictured: her sweet temper never knew a cloud; her rare grace and exquisite beauty had not forsaken her; the suspicion I had once harboured now seemed forgotten, or came back to me only like the remembrance of an evil dream, and yet, and yet I could not say that I loved my wife. Sometimes I thought my depression was caused by a secret malady undermining my existence, for I was now often afflicted by headache and lassitude.

Not very long after I had begun to note these symptoms, which I was careful to conceal from my wife, I woke one morning with a dull, throbbing sensation in my brain. I noticed a peculiar odour in the room which appeared to make the air so heavy that it was a labour to breathe: it was a familiar odour, but not musk, lavender, attar of roses, or any of the perfumes Rosaura was so fond of, and I could not remember what it was. For an hour I lay on my bed disinclined to rise, vainly trying to recall the name of the scent, and with a vague fear that my memory was beginning to fail, that I was perhaps even sinking into hopeless imbecility. A few weeks later it all happened again—the late waking, the oppressive sensation, the faint familiar odour in the room. Again and again the same thing occurred. I was anxious and my health suffered, but my suspicions were now thoroughly aroused. In Rosaura's absence I searched the apartment. I found many scent-bottles, but the odour I was in quest of was not there. A small ebony silver-bound box I could not open, having no key to fit it, and I dared not break the lock, for I had now grown afraid of my wife. My evanescent passion had utterly passed away by this time; hatred had taken its place—fear and hatred, for these two ever go together. I dissembled well. I feigned illness; when she kissed me I smiled while loathing her in my heart; the folds of a serpent would have been more endurable than her arms about me, yet I affected to sleep peacefully in her bosom.

One day while out riding I dropped my whip; dismounting to pick it up I put my foot on a small dark green plant with long lance-shaped leaves and clusters of greenish-white flowers. It is a plant well known for its powerful narcotic smell and for the acrid milky juice the stem gives out when bruised.

"This is it!" I cried in exultation. "This is the mysterious perfume I have been seeking. From this little thing I will advance to great things."

I resolved to follow the clue; but I would be secret in all I did, like a man advancing to strike a venomous snake and fearing to rouse it before he is ready to deliver the blow.

Taking a sprig of the plant I went to an old herdsman living on my estate and asked him its name.

He shook his head. "Old Salomé the *curandera,* knows everything," he answered. "She can tell you the virtue of every plant, cure diseases, and prophesy many things."

I replied that I was sorry she knew so much, and rode home determined to visit her.

Close to the Espinillo house there existed a group of little ranchos, tenanted by some very poor people who were charitably allowed by Roldan to live and keep a few cattle rent free on his land. In one of these huts lived

Salomé, the *curandera*. I had often heard
about her, for all her neighbours, not even
excepting my father-in-law, professed to believe in her skill; but I had never seen her,
having always felt a great contempt for these
ignorant but cunning people, who give themselves mysterious airs and pretend to know so
much more than their neighbours. In my
trouble, however, I forgot my prejudice and
hastened to consult her. On first entering her
hovel, I was astonished to discover in Salomé
the old woman I had seen in the tala wood on
my arrival at the Espinillo. I sat down on
the bleached skull of a horse—the only seat
she had to offer me—and began by saying
that I had long known her by fame, but now
desired a more intimate acquaintance. She
thanked me dryly. I spoke of medicinal
herbs, and, drawing from my pocket a leaf
of the strange-smelling plant I had provided
for the occasion, asked her what she called it.

" 'Tis the Flor de Pesadilla," she replied,
and, seeing me start, she cackled maliciously.

I tried to laugh off my nervousness. "What
a pity to give a pretty flower a name so terrible!" I said. "The *night-mare flower*—only
a madman could have called it that! Perhaps

you can tell me why it was called by such a name?"

She answered that she did not know, then angrily added "that I came to her like one wishing to steal knowledge."

"No," I returned, "tell me, mother, all I wish to know, and I will give you this;" and with that I drew from my pocket a gold doubloon.

Her eyes sparkled like fireflies at the sight. "What do you wish to know, my son?" she asked in eager tones.

I replied, "Out of this flower there comes by night an evil spirit and cruelly persecutes me. I do not wish to fly from it. Give me strength to resist it, for it drowns my senses in slumber."

The old hag became strangely excited at my words; she jumped up clapping her hands, then burst into a peal of laughter so shrill and unearthly that my blood was chilled in my veins, and the hair stood up on my head. Finally she sank down in a crouching attitude upon the floor, mumbling, and with a horrid expression of gratified malice in her eyes.

"Ah, sister mine!" I heard her mutter. "Ah, bright eyes, sweet lips, because of you I was driven out, and those who knew and obeyed me before you were born now neglect and despise me. Insolent wretch! Fools, fools that they were! See now what you have done; something must surely come of this, something good for me. She was always bold, the pretty one, now she grows careless."

She kept on in this way for some time, occasionally uttering a little cackling laugh. I was greatly disturbed at her words; and she, too, when the excitement had worn itself out, seemed troubled in mind, and from time to time stole an anxious glance at the great yellow coin in my hand.

At length she roused herself, and taking a small wooden crucifix from the wall approached me.

"My son," she said, "I know all your afflictions, and that you are now only about to increase them. Nevertheless, I cannot reject the succour Heaven in its infinite compassion sends to one so old and feeble. Kneel, my son, and swear on this cross that whatever happens to you you will never disclose this visit, or name my name to that infamous despiser of her betters, that accursed viper with a pretty face—alas, what am I saying? I am old—old, my son, and sometimes my mind wanders. I mean your sweet wife, your pretty angel, Rosaura; swear that she shall never know of this visit; for to you she is sweet and good and beautiful, to every one she is good, only to me —a poor old woman—she is more bitter than the wild pumpkin, more cruel than the hungry hawk!"

I went down on my knees and took the required oath. "Go now," she said, "and return to me before sunset."

On my return to the hovel the old woman gave me a bundle of leaves, apparently just gathered and hastily dried by the fire. "Take these," she said, "and keep them where no eye can see them. Every night, before retiring, chew well and swallow two or three of them."

"Will they prevent sleep?" I asked.

"No, no," said the hag, with a little cackle as she clutched the doubloon; "they will not keep you long awake when there is nothing stirring. When you smell Pesadilla be careful to keep your eyes closed, and you will dream strange dreams."

I shuddered at her words and went home. I followed her directions, and every night after chewing the leaves felt strangely wakeful; not feverish, but with senses clear and keen. This would last for about two hours, then I would sleep quietly till morning.

Close to the head of the bed, on a small table, there was an ebony cross on which a golden Christ was suspended, and it was Rosaura's habit every night after undressing to kneel before it and perform her devotions. One night, about a fortnight after I had seen Salomé, while I lay with partially closed eyes, I noticed that Rosaura glanced frequently towards me. She rose, and moving stealthily about undressed herself, then came, as was her custom, and knelt down beside the bed. Presently she placed a hand gently on mine and whispered, "Asleep, Pelino?" Receiving no reply she raised her other hand, there was a small phial in it, and removing the stopper the room was quickly filled with the powerful Pesadilla odour. She bent over me, placing the phial close to my nose, then poured a few clammy drops into my lips, and withdrew from the bedside uttering a great sigh of relief. The drug produced no effect on me: on the contrary, I felt intensely wakeful, and watched her slightest movement, while outwardly I was calm and apparently in a sound sleep.

Rosaura retired to a seat beside the dressing-table at some distance from the bed. She smiled to herself and appeared to be in a soft, placid frame of mind. By-and-by she opened the small ebony box I have already spoken about, and took from it a little clay pot and placed it on the table before her. Suddenly I heard a rushing noise like the sound of great wings above me; then it seemed to me as if beings of some kind had alighted on the roof; the walls shook, and I heard voices calling, "Sister! sister!" Rosaura rose and threw off her night-dress, then, taking ointment from the pot and rubbing it on the palms of her hands, she passed it rapidly over her whole body, arms, and legs, only leaving her face untouched. Instantly she became covered with a plumage of a slaty-blue colour, only on her face there were no feathers. At the same time from her shoulders sprang wings which were incessantly agitated. She hurried forth, closing the door after her; once more the walls trembled or seemed to tremble; a sound of rushing wings was heard, and, mingling with it, shrill peals of laughter; then all was still. At the last, in my amazement and horror, I had forgotten myself and stared with wide-open eyes at her doings; but in her haste she went out without one glance at me.

Since my interview with the *curandera* the suspicion, already then in my mind, that my wife was one of those abhorred beings possessing superhuman knowledge, which they kept secret and doubtless used for evil purposes, had grown into a settled conviction. And now that I had satisfied the dangerous curiosity that had animated me, had actually seen my wife making use of her horrid occult arts, what was I to do? Not even yet was my curiosity wholly satisfied, however, and to inspire me to further action the hatred I had long nursed in secret became all at once a bitter, burning desire for vengeance on the woman who had linked with mine her accursed destiny. I was desperate now and fearless, and anxious to be up and doing. Suddenly a strange thought came to me, and springing to my feet I tore off my shirt and began to rub myself with the ointment. The mysterious effect was produced on me—I was instantly covered with dark blue feathers, and on my shoulders I felt

wings. Perhaps, I thought, I am now like
those abhorred beings in soul also. But the
thought scarcely troubled me, for I was insane
with rage. Catching up a slender rapier that
hung on the wall, I sallied forth. The moon
had risen, and the night was almost as bright
as day. I felt strangely buoyant as I walked,
and could scarcely keep my feet on the ground.
I raised my pinions, and rose without appar-
ent effort perpendicularly to a vast height in
the air. I heard a shrill peal of laughter near
me, then a winged being like myself shot by
me with a celerity compared with which the
falcon's flight is slow. I followed, and the
still night air was like a mighty rushing wind
in my face. I glanced back for a moment to
see the Verro, like a silver thread, far, far beneath me. Behind me in the northern sky
shone the cluster of the seven stars, for we flew
towards the Magellanic clouds. We passed
over vast desert pampas, over broad rivers and
mountain ranges of which I had never heard.
My guide vanished before me, still I kept on
—the same stars shining in my face. Shrill
peals of laughter were occasionally heard, and
dark forms were seen shooting past me. And
now I noticed them sweeping downwards to-

wards the distant earth. Beneath me lay a
vast lake, and in its centre an island, its shores
covered with a dense forest of tall trees; but
the interior was a lofty plain, barren and desolate. To this plain the flying forms de-
scended, I with them, still grasping the naked
weapon in my hand. I alighted in the middle of a city surrounded by a wall. It was all
dark and silent, and the houses were of stone
and vast in size, each house standing by itself
surrounded by broad stony walks. The sight
of these great gloomy buildings, the work of
former times, inspired my soul with awe, almost with fear, and for a short time banished
the thought of Rosaura. But I did not feel
astonished. From childhood I had been
taught to believe in the existence of this often
and vainly sought city in the wilderness,
founded centuries ago by the Bishop of
Placentia and his missionary colonists, but
probably no longer the habitation of Christian men. The account history gives of it, the
hundred traditions I had heard, the fate of
the expeditions sent out for its discovery, and
the horror the Indian tribes manifest concerning it, all seemed to indicate that some powerful influence of an unearthly maleficent nature

rests upon it. The very elements appear leagued together to protect it from prying curiosity, if there is any foundation for the common belief that on the approach of white men the earth trembles, the waters of the lake rise up in huge billows covering the shores with angry foam, while the sky darkens overhead, and sudden flashes of lightning reveal gigantic human forms in the clouds. The explorer turns in terror and dismay from this evil region, called by the Indians *Trapalanda*.

For a few moments I stood still in a wide silent street; but very soon I discerned a crowd of winged people hurrying towards me, talking and laughing aloud, and, to escape them, I concealed myself in the shadow of a vast arched entrance to one of the buildings. In a moment they entered after me, and passed into the interior of the building without seeing me. My courage returned, and I followed them at some distance. The passage led me quickly into a vast room, so long that it looked like a wide avenue of stone arched over. Around me all was dark and deserted, but at the further end of the room, which seemed nearly half a mile from me, there was a great light and a crowd of people. They were

whirling about, apparently dancing, all the
time shouting and laughing like maniacs.
The group I had followed had probably already joined this crowd, for I could not see
them. Walls, floor, and the high arched roof
were all of black stone. There were no fires
or lamps, but on the walls were painted figures of jaguars, horses speeding through clouds
of dust, Indians engaged in fight with white
men, serpents, whirlwinds, grassy plains on
fire, with ostriches flying before the flames, and
a hundred other things; the men and animals
were drawn life size, and the bright colours
they were painted in gave out a phospho-
rescent light, making them visible and shedding a dim twilight into the room. I advanced cautiously, rapier in hand, and keeping
always in the centre of the floor where it was
very dark, being at least ten yards from the
pictured walls on either hand. At length I
came on a black figure crouching on the floor
before me; at the sound of my step it started
up—a great gaunt man, with cavernous eyes
that gleamed like will-o'-wisps, and a white
beard reaching to his waist. His sole garment
was a piece of guanaco hide tied round the
body, and his yellow skin was drawn so closely

over his bones that he looked more like a skeleton than a living being. As I approached
him I noticed an iron chain on his ankle, and
feeling now very bold and careless, and com-
miserating this sad object, I said, "Old man,
what brought you here? We are comrades in
misfortune; shall I give you liberty?" For a
few moments he stared at me with a wild,
astonished look, then bending forward till his
lips almost touched my face, he murmured,
"This is hell—do you not know? How can
you get out of it? Look!" and his finger
pointed over my shoulder. "Poor old man,
your mind is gone!" I said. He answered
nothing, but dropped down on his face upon
the floor again. The next moment I saw at my
elbow a woman, all feathered like myself,
who stood staring at me with an expression of
amazement and fear in her face. As I turned
she uttered a piercing yell; I raised my
weapon, but she fled screaming beyond its
reach. The old man lifted his head again
and stared at me, then pointed towards the
door by which I had entered. In another moment such a shrill and outrageous hubbub re-
sounded from the further end of the room that,
struck with sudden terror, I turned and fled.

Before I reached the door a crowd of feathered women appeared before me, all staring at me with pale, furious faces; but the cries behind me were coming nearer; there was no other way of escape, and I rushed at them striking them furiously with my rapier. I saw distinctly one woman fall before its thrust, while three or four more were borne down by the shock of my body. I passed out over them, sprang into the air, and fled. The shrill angry cries beneath me quickly died away; I was at a vast height speeding towards the cluster of the seven stars. In the homeward flight I was alone in the vast solitary sky, for not one dark winged form did I meet, nor did any sound break the deep silence. In about two hours I was again in my own district, and saw far beneath me the Verro glimmering in the moonlight.

I reached my home and re-entered my silent room, where the candle still burnt on the dressing-table just where Rosaura had left it. I now began to experience a terrible excitement, for every moment I expected the return of my wife. Cautiously I disposed everything just as she had left it. I had forgotten for a time the wings and feathers that clothed my body.

Merciful heaven! what should I do to rid myself of them? I tore at the feathers with my hands, but they were deeply embedded in the flesh. Perhaps, I thought, when daylight comes they will go off of themeslves. Night was wearing away; in an agony of fear I concealed myself under the bed-clothes. All my desperate courage had now left me; I was completely at Rosaura's mercy, and no doubt she would wreak some dreadful vengeance on me. In this miserable condition I lay for another hour. Still she came not, and every moment my terror and anguish increased until it was almost more than I could bear. Suddenly a sound was heard—a sound of rushing wings; a few moments later I heard the cautious footsteps of several people in the room adjoining mine. Then I heard voices whispering. "Leave me now, sisters," one said. "Yes, sister," another replied; "but remember it is late, be quick, and if it cannot be concealed say it was an accident—a dream—that he did it, anything to save yourself." Then all was silent. Slowly the door opened. A sweat of terror broke over my forehead. I closed my eyes. I was about to rise in my distraction, and throw myself at once on the devilish mercy of my wife. I looked again and saw her standing in the room with a face like ashes, her legs trembling under her, and the blood oozing from her bosom. She staggered to a seat, gasping for breath; with trembling hands she again opened the small ebony box and took from it a second clay pot. Taking ointment from it she rubbed herself with it. Slowly she passed her hands downward from her shoulders, and lo, the feathers withered up and disappeared, but the blood continued to flow from her wounded breast. She took up a garment lying near, and tried to staunch it. I forgot everything in the horror and fascination that possessed my soul. I had risen to a sitting position, and was staring at her with wide-open eyes when she glanced towards me. She sprang from her seat uttering a terrified shriek, then fell back with a groan upon the floor. For some time I dared not approach her, but she never stirred. I heard footsteps in the next room; then there was a knock at the door, and my servants calling. I perceived the danger of my position. I flew to the door and locked it. "Go back to bed," I cried; "your mistress has had a bad dream, that's all!" The servants retired. I quickly applied ointment from the second pot to my body, and was restored to my former state.   I examined Rosaura and found that she was dead.   It was a horrible death she had met; still I felt no compassion, no remorse, though convinced that my own hand had inflicted her death-wound.   I dressed myself and sat down to meditate on my situation.   Day had long dawned, and the sun shining in that ghastly chamber reminded me of the necessity of action.   There at my feet lay my wife, an expression of horror and anguish still disfiguring her beautiful countenance, the blood still slowly oozing from her wounded breast. But in my heart there was now a great despair that rendered me incapable of making any resolution.   What would the world say when it came to look into that blood-stained chamber?   Should I fly to escape the fate of a murderer?   It was late for that; moreover, my flight would proclaim me guilty at once, and I was not guilty.   I should be captured and put to a death most horrible.   Or would it do to tell the simple truth; to say, when interrogated, "I am guilty, yet not guilty," and then proceed to relate the marvellous circumstances?   Would such a story be believed?

Perhaps yes, but that would avail me nothing: the prosecuting counsel—for a trial for murder would certainly come—would say that I had a good invention, and was learned in legends and superstitions, and no judge would have the courage to acquit me.

I was still sitting, unable to decide on anything, when I heard voices eagerly talking, footsteps rapidly approaching, then a loud rap at my door. It was my father-in-law come to surprise us by an early visit. I recognised his voice, though it was full of alarm, for the servants had already told him what they had heard. I was about to rise and admit him, since further concealment was impossible, when the frail lock gave way, and the door flew wide open. Roldan stared in, horror-struck, for some moments, while loud exclamations escaped from the servants standing behind him. "Rosaura—O my beloved daughter!" cried the old man at last, "dead—slain! In the name of God, Pelino, explain this!"

I will tell him that in a sudden fit of rage she stabbed herself, I thought; then immediately I perceived that this story would not do, for no person had ever seen Rosaura in a passion. Roldan marked my hesitation. "Assassin!" he shrieked, springing forward and seizing my arm with a firm grip. In an instant an uncontrollable rage possessed me, and all prudence was forgotten. I rose, shaking him violently from me. "Back!" I cried. "Know, miserable dotard, that this is your work! When I had escaped from your detestable daughter's wiles, who but you dragged me back to her? Accursed be the day in which I first saw you and this fiend with a beautiful mask! This is the result of your interference!" By giving vent to these frantic words I had destroyed myself, for they almost amounted to a confession of guilt. Overwhelmed with despair, I threw myself once more on my seat. Roldan fell back to the door, hurriedly dispatched one of my servants to summon the Alcalde, and took measures to prevent me from escaping.

The Alcalde soon arrived; I was formally charged and sent to Buenos Ayres; the trial and sentence followed. Nothing that could be urged in my defence was omitted, but all in vain. Had I, at the proper moment, feigned a grief I did not feel, and told the story my defender afterwards invented to account for Rosaura's death, I should have been saved. But after my behaviour towards my father-in-law, when he entered that chamber of death, nothing could avail me. That anything will now interpose between me and the fatal *banquillo* I have no hope.

Before long my family will hear of my fate, and this is a great bitterness for me: it is for them I write this narrative; when they read it they will know that I was no murderer. Accidentally I set my heel on the head of a venomous serpent, and crushed it—that was my only crime.

It is hard to die so young, but life could no longer be sweet and pleasant to me as in former days. Sometimes, lying awake at night, thinking of the great breezy plains, till I almost fancy I hear the cattle lowing far off, and the evening call of the partridge, the tears gush from my eyes. It would be sad to live far away from that sweet life I knew, to wander amongst strangers in distant lands, always haunted by the memory of that tragedy.

I have told my story to my Father Confessor, and I know from the strange look in his face that he does not altogether believe it, and thinks, perhaps, that at the last I will declare it all an invention.   When I am on the bench, and the bandage is on my eyes; when the muskets are levelled at my breast, and he is forced at the last to quit my side, then he will know that I have told him the truth; for who could willingly die with the burden of a great crime on his soul?

Let him, in justice to me, write here at the end of this confession, before sending it to my unhappy father in Portugal, whether he believes that I have spoken the truth.

NIÑO DIABLO

NIÑO DIABLO

THE wide pampa rough with long grass;
a vast level disc now growing dark,
the horizon encircling it with a ring as fault-
less as that made by a pebble dropped into
smooth water; above it the clear sky of June,
wintry and pale, still showing in the west the
saffron hues of the afterglow tinged with
vapoury violet and grey. In the centre of
the disc a large low rancho thatched with
yellow rushes, a few stunted trees and cattle
enclosures grouped about it; and dimly seen
in the shadows, cattle and sheep reposing. At
the gate stands Gregory Gorostiaga, lord of
house, lands and ruminating herds, leisurely
unsaddling his horse; for whatsoever Gregory
does is done leisurely. Although no person
is within earshot he talks much over his task,
now rebuking his restive animal, and now
cursing his benumbed fingers and the hard
knots in his gear. A curse falls readily and
not without a certain natural grace from
Gregory's lips; it is the oiled feather with

which he touches every difficult knot encountered in life. From time to time he glances towards the open kitchen door, from which issue the far-flaring light of the fire and familiar voices, with savoury smells of cookery that come to his nostrils like pleasant messengers.

The unsaddling over at last the freed horse gallops away, neighing joyfully, to seek his fellows; but Gregory is not a four-footed thing to hurry himself; and so, stepping slowly and pausing frequently to look about him as if reluctant to quit the cold night air, he turns towards the house.

The spacious kitchen was lighted by two or three wicks in cups of melted fat, and by a great fire in the middle of the clay floor that cast crowds of dancing shadows on the walls and filled the whole room with grateful warmth. On the walls were fastened many deers' heads, and on their convenient prongs were hung bridles and lassos, ropes of onions and garlics, bunches of dried herbs, and various other objects. At the fire a piece of beef was roasting on a spit; and in a large pot suspended by hook and chain from the smoke-blackened central beam, boiled and bubbled an ocean of mutton broth, puffing out white

clouds of steam redolent of herbs and cumin-
seed. Close to the fire, skimmer in hand, sat
Magdalen, Gregory's fat and florid wife, engaged in frying pies in a second smaller pot.
There also, on a high, straight-backed chair,
sat Ascension, her sister-in-law, a wrinkled
spinster; also, in a low rush-bottomed seat,
her mother-in-law, an ancient white-headed
dame, staring vacantly into the flames. On
the other side of the fire were Gregory's two
eldest daughters, occupied just now in serving
maté to their elders—that harmless bitter
decoction the sipping of which fills up all vacant moments from dawn to bed-time—pretty
dove-eyed girls of sixteen, both also named
Magdalen, but not after their mother nor because confusion was loved by the family for its
own sake; they were twins, and born on the
day sacred to Santa Magdalena. Slumbering
dogs and cats were disposed about the floor,
also four children. The eldest, a boy, sitting
with legs outstretched before him, was cutting
threads from a slip of colt's hide looped over
his great toe. The two next, boy and girl,
were playing a simple game called nines, once
known to English children as nine men's mor-
rice; the lines were rudely scratched on the

clay floor, and the men they played with were bits of hardened clay, nine red and as many white. The youngest, a girl of five, sat on the flour nursing a kitten that purred contentedly on her lap and drowsily winked its blue eyes at the fire; and as she swayed herself from side to side she lisped out the old lullaby in her baby voice:—

A-ro-ró mi niño
A-ro-ró mi sol,
A-ro-ró pedazos
De mi corazon.

Gregory stood on the threshold surveying this domestic scene with manifest pleasure.

"Papa mine, what have you brought me?" cried the child with the kitten.

"Brought you, interested? Stiff whiskers and cold hands to pinch your dirty little cheeks. How is your cold to-night, mother?"

"Yes, son, it is very cold to-night; we knew that before you came in," replied the old dame testily as she drew her chair a little closer to the fire.

"It is useless speaking to her," remarked Ascension. "With her to be out of temper is to be deaf."

"What has happened to put her out?" he asked.

"I can tell you papa," cried one of the twins. "She wouldn't let me make your cigars to-day, and sat down out of doors to make them herself. It was after breakfast when the sun was warm."

"And of course she fell asleep," chimed in Ascension.

"Let me tell it, auntie!" exclaimed the other. "And she fell asleep, and in a moment Rosita's lamb came and ate up the whole of the tobacco-leaf in her lap."

"It didn't!" cried Rosita, looking up from her game. "I opened its mouth and looked with all my eyes, and there was no tobacco-leaf in it."

"That lamb! that lamb!" said Gregory slily. "Is it to be wondered at that we are turning grey before our time—all except Rosita! Remind me to-morrow, wife, to take it to the flock; or if it has grown fat on all the tobacco-leaf, aprons and old shoes it has eaten—"

"Oh no, no, no!" screamed Rosita, starting up and throwing the game into confusion, just when her little brother had made a row and was in the act of seizing on one of her pieces in triumph.

"Hush, silly child, he will not harm your lamb," said the mother, pausing from her task and raising eyes that were tearful with the smoke of the fire and of the cigarette she held between her good-humoured lips. "And now, if these children have finished speaking of their important affairs, tell me, Gregory, what news do you bring?"

"They say," he returned, sitting down and taking the maté-cup from his daughter's hand, "that the invading Indians bring seven hundred lances, and that those that first opposed them were all slain. Some say they are now retreating with the cattle they have taken; while others maintain that they are waiting to fight our men."

"Oh, my sons, my sons, what will happen to them!" cried Magdalen, bursting into tears.

"Why do you cry, wife, before God gives you cause?" returned her husband. "Are not all men born to fight the infidel? Our boys are not alone—all their friends and neighbours are with them."

"Say not this to me, Gregory, for I am not a fool nor blind. All their friends indeed!

And this very day I have seen the Niño Diablo; he galloped past the house, whistling like a partridge that knows no care. Why must my two sons be called away, while he, a youth without occupation and with no mother to cry for him, remains behind?"

"You talk folly, Magdalen," replied her lord. "Complain that the ostrich and puma are more favoured than your sons, since no man calls on them to serve the state; but mention not the Niño, for he is freer than the wild things which Heaven has made, and fights not on this side nor on that."

"Coward! Miserable!" murmured the incensed mother.

Whereupon one of the twins flushed scarlet, and retorted, "He is not a coward, mother!"

"And if not a coward why does he sit on the hearth among women and old men in times like these? Grieved am I to hear a daughter of mine speak in defence of one who is a vagabond and a stealer of other men's horses!"

The girl's eyes flashed angrily, but she answered not a word.

"Hold your tongue, woman, and accuse no man of crimes," spoke Gregory. "Let every Christian take proper care of his animals; and

as for the infidel's horses, he is a virtuous man
that steals them. The girl speaks truth; the
Niño is no coward, but he fights not with our
weapons. The web of the spider is coarse and
ill-made compared with the snare he spreads
to entangle his prey." Thus fixing his eyes
on the face of the girl who had spoken, he
added: "Therefore be warned in season, my
daughter, and fall not into the snare of the
Niño Diablo."

Again the girl blushed and hung her head.

At this moment a clatter of hoofs, the jan-
gling of a bell, and shouts of a traveller to the
horses driven before him, came in at the open
door. The dogs roused themselves, almost
overturning the children in their hurry to rush
out; and up rose Gregory to find out who was
approaching with so much noise.

"I know, *papita,*" cried one of the children.
"It is Uncle Polycarp."

"You are right, child," said her father.
"Cousin Polycarp always arrives at night,
shouting to his animals like a troop of Indians." And with that he went out to welcome his boisterous relative.

The traveller soon arrived, spurring his
horse, scared at the light and snorting loudly,

to within two yards of the door. In a few minutes the saddle was thrown off, the fore feet of the bellmare fettered, and the horses allowed to wander away in quest of pasturage; then the two men turned into the kitchen.

A short, burly man aged about fifty, wearing a soft hat thrust far back on his head, with truculent greenish eyes beneath arched bushy eyebrows, and a thick shapeless nose surmounting a bristly moustache—such was Cousin Polycarp. From neck to feet he was covered with a blue cloth poncho, and on his heels he wore enormous silver spurs that clanked and jangled over the floor like the fetters of a convict. After greeting the women and bestowing the avuncular blessing on the children, who had clamoured for it as for some inestimable boon—he sat down, and flinging back his poncho displayed at his waist a huge silver-hilted knife and a heavy brass-barrelled horse-pistol.

"Heaven he praised for its goodness, Cousin Magdalen," he said. "What with pies and spices your kitchen is more fragrant than a garden of flowers. That's as it should be, for nothing but rum have I tasted this bleak day. And the boys are away fighting, Gregory tells me. Good! When the eaglets have found out their wings let them try their talons. What, Cousin Magdalen, crying for the boys! Would you have had them girls?"

"Yes, a thousand times," she replied, drying her wet eyes on her apron.

"Ah, Magdalen, daughters can't be always young and sweet-tempered, like your brace of pretty partridges yonder. They grow old, Cousin Magdalen—old and ugly and spiteful; and are more bitter and worthless than the wild pumpkin. But I speak not of those who are present, for I would say nothing to offend my respected cousin Ascension, whom may God preserve, though she never married."

"Listen to me, Cousin Polycarp," returned the insulted dame so pointedly alluded to. "Say nothing to me nor of me, and I will also hold my peace concerning you; for you know very well that if I were disposed to open my lips I could say a thousand things."

"Enough, enough, you have already said them a thousand times," he interrupted. "I know all that, cousin; let us say no more."

"That is only what I ask," she retorted, "for I have never loved to bandy words with you; and you know already, therefore I need not recall it to your mind, that if I am single it is not because some men whose names I could mention if I felt disposed—and they are the names not of dead but of living men—would not have been glad to marry me; but because I preferred my liberty and the goods I inherited from my father; and I see not what advantage there is in being the wife of one who is a brawler and a drunkard and spender of other people's money, and I know not what besides."

"There it is!" said Polycarp, appealing to the fire. "I knew that I had thrust my foot into a red ant's nest—careless that I am! But in truth, Ascension, it was fortunate for you in those distant days you mention that you hardened your heart against all lovers. For wives, like cattle that must be branded with their owner's mark, are first of all taught submission to their husbands; and consider, cousin, what tears! what sufferings!" And having ended thus abruptly, he planted his elbows on his knees and busied himself with the cigarette he had been trying to roll up with his cold drunken fingers for the last five minutes.

Ascension gave a nervous twitch at the red

cotton kerchief on her head, and cleared her throat with a sound "sharp and short like the shrill swallow's cry," when——

"*Madre del Cielo,* how you frightened me!" screamed one of the twins, giving a great start.

The cause of this sudden outcry was discovered in the presence of a young man quietly seated on the bench at the girl's side. He had not been there a minute before, and no person had seen him enter the room—what wonder that the girl was startled! He was slender in form, and had small hands and feet, and oval olive face, smooth as a girl's except for the incipient moustache on his lip. In place of a hat he wore only a scarlet ribbon bound about his head, to keep back the glossy black hair that fell to his shoulders; and he was wrapped in a white woollen Indian poncho, while his lower limbs were cased in white colt-skin coverings, shaped like stockings to his feet, with the red tassels of his embroidered garters falling to the ankles.

"The Niño Diablo!" all cried in a breath, the children manifesting the greatest joy at his appearance. But old Gregory spoke with affected anger. "Why do you always drop on us in this treacherous way, like rain through a leaky thatch?" he exclaimed. "Keep these strange arts for your visits in the infidel country; here we are all Christians, and praise God on the threshold when we visit a neighbour's house. And now, Niño Diablo, what news of the Indians?"

"Nothing do I know and little do I concern myself about specks on the horizon," returned the visitor with a light laugh. And at once all the children gathered round him, for the Niño they considered to belong to them when he came, and not to their elders with their solemn talk about Indian warfare and lost horses. And now, now he would finish that wonderful story, long in the telling, of the little girl alone and lost in the great desert, and surrounded by all the wild animals met to discuss what they should do with her. It was a grand story, even mother Magdalen listened, though she pretended all the time to be thinking only of her pies—and the teller, like the grand old historians of other days, put most eloquent speeches, all made out of his own head, into the lips (and beaks) of the various actors—puma, ostrich, deer, cavy, and the rest.

In the midst of this performance supper was
announced, and all gathered willingly round a
dish of Magdalen's pies, filled with minced
meat, hard-boiled eggs chopped small, raisins,
and plenty of spice.   After the pies came
roast beef; and, finally, great basins of mutton
broth fragrant with herbs and cumin-seed.
The rage of hunger satisfied, each one said a
prayer, the elders murmuring with bowed
heads, the children on their knees uplifting
shrill voices.   Then followed the concluding
semi-religious ceremony of the day, when each
child in its turn asked a blessing of father,
mother, grandmother, uncle, aunt, and not
omitting the stranger within the gates, even
the Niño Diablo of evil-sounding name.

The men drew forth their pouches, and
began making their cigarettes, when once more
the children gathered round the story-teller,
their faces glowing with expectation.

"No, no," cried their mother.   "No more
stories to-night—to bed, to bed!"

"Oh, mother, mother!" cried Rosita plead-
ingly, and struggling to free herself; for the
good woman had dashed in among them to
enforce obedience.   "Oh, let me stay till the
story ends!   The reed-cat has said such things!

Oh, what will they do with the poor little girl?"

"And oh, mother mine!" drowsily sobbed her little sister; "the armadillo that said—that said nothing because it had nothing to say, and the partridge that whistled and said,—" and here she broke into a prolonged wail. The boys also added their voices until the hubbub was no longer to be borne, and Gregory rose up in his wrath and called on some one to lend him a big whip; only then they yielded, and still sobbing and casting many a lingering look behind, were led from the kitchen.

During this scene the Niño had been carrying on a whispered conversation with the pretty Magdalen of his choice, heedless of the uproar of which he had been the indirect cause; deaf also to the bitter remarks of Ascension concerning some people who, having no homes of their own, were fond of coming uninvited into other people's houses, only to repay the hospitality extended to them by stealing their silly daughters' affections, and teaching their children to rebel against their authority.

But the noise and confusion had served to arouse Polycarp from a drowsy fit; for like a boa constrictor, he had dined largely after his long fast, and dinner had made him dull; bending towards his cousin he whispered earnestly: "Who is this young stranger, Gregory?"

"In what corner of the earth have you been hiding to ask who the Niño Diablo is?" returned the other.

"Must I know the history of every cat and dog?"

"The Niño is not cat nor dog, cousin, but a man among men, like a falcon among birds. When a child of six the Indians killed all his relations and carried him into captivity. After five years he escaped out of their hands, and, guided by sun and stars and signs on the earth, he found his way back to the Christian's country, bringing many beautiful horses stolen from his captors; also the name of Niño Diablo first given to him by the infidel. We know him by no other."

"This is a good story; in truth I like it well —it pleases me mightily," said Polycarp. "And what more, cousin Gregory?"

"More than I can tell, cousin. When he comes the dogs bark not—who knows why? his tread is softer than the cat's; the untamed

horse is tame for him. Always in the midst
of dangers, yet no harm, no scratch. Why?
Because he stoops like the falcon, makes his
stroke and is gone—Heaven knows where!"

"What strange things are you telling me?
Wonderful! And what more, cousin Gregory?"

"He often goes into the Indian country, and
lives freely with the infidel, disguised, for they
do not know him who was once their captive.
They speak of the Niño Diablo to him, saying
that when they catch that thief they will flay
him alive. He listens to their strange stories,
then leaves them, taking their finest ponchos
and silver ornaments, and the flower of their
horses."

"A brave youth, one after my own heart,
cousin Gregory. Heaven defend and prosper
him in all his journeys into the Indian territory! Before we part I shall embrace him
and offer him my friendship, which is worth
something. More, tell me more, cousin
Gregory?"

"These things I tell you to put you on your
guard; look well to your horses, cousin."

"What!" shouted the other, lifting himself
up from his stooping posture, and staring at

his relation with astonishment and kindling anger in his countenance.

The conversation had been carried on in a low tone, and the sudden loud exclamation startled them all—all except the Niño, who continued smoking and chatting pleasantly to the twins.

"Lightning and pestilence, what is this you say to me, Gregory Gorostiaga!" continued Polycarp, violently slapping his thigh and thrusting his hat farther back on his head.

"Prudence!" whispered Gregory. "Say nothing to offend the Niño, he never forgives an enemy—with horses."

"Talk not to me of prudence!" bawled the other. "You hit me on the apple of the eye and counsel me not to cry out. What! have not I, whom men call Polycarp of the South, wrestled with tigers in the desert, and must I hold my peace because of a boy—even a boy devil? Talk of what you like, cousin, and I am a meek man—meek as a sucking babe; but touch not on my horses, for then I am a whirl-wind, a conflagration, a river flooded in winter, and all wrath and destruction like an invasion of Indians! Who can stand before me? Ribs of steel are no protection! Look at my knife; do you ask why there are stains on the blade? Listen; because it has gone straight to the robber's heart!" And with that he drew out his great knife and flourished it wildly, and made stabs and slashes at an imaginary foe suspended above the fire.

The pretty girls grew silent and pale and trembled like poplar leaves; the old grandmother rose up, and clutching at her shawl toddled hurriedly away, while Ascension uttered a snort of disdain. But the Niño still talked and smiled, blowing thin smoke-clouds from his lips, careless of that tempest of wrath gathering before him; till, seeing the other so calm, the man of war returned his weapon to its sheath, and glancing round and lowering his voice to a conversational tone, informed his hearers that his name was Polycarp, one known and feared by all men,—especially in the south; that he was disposed to live in peace and amity with the entire human race, and he therefore considered it unreasonable of some men to follow him about the world asking him to kill them. "Perhaps," he concluded, with a touch of irony, "they think I gain something by putting them to death. A mistake, good friends; I gain nothing by it!

I am not a vulture, and their dead bodies can be of no use to me."

Just after this sanguinary protest and disclaimer the Niño all at once made a gesture as if to impose silence, and turned his face towards the door, his nostrils dilating, and his eyes appearing to grow large and luminous like those of a cat.

"What do you hear, Niño?" asked Gregory.

"I hear lapwings screaming," he replied.

"Only at a fox perhaps," said the other. "But go to the door, Niño, and listen."

"No need," he returned, dropping his hand, the light of a sudden excitement passing from his face.   " 'Tis only a single horseman riding this way at a fast gallop."

Polycarp got up and went to the door, saying that when a man was among robbers it behoved him to look well after his cattle. Then he came back and sat down again. "Perhaps," he remarked, with a side glance at the Niño, "a better plan would be to watch the thief. A lie, cousin Gregory; no lapwings are screaming; no single horseman approaching at a fast gallop. The night is serene, and earth as silent as the sepulchre."

"Prudence!" whispered Gregory again.

"Ah, cousin, always playful like a kitten; when will you grow old and wise? Can you not see a sleeping snake without turning aside to stir it up with your naked foot?"

Strange to say, Polycarp made no reply. A long experience in getting up quarrels had taught him that these impassive men were, in truth, often enough like venomous snakes, quick and deadly when roused. He became secret and watchful in his manner.

All now were intently listening. Then said Gregory, "Tell us, Niño, what voices, fine as the trumpet of the smallest fly, do you hear coming from that great silence? Has the mother skunk put her little ones to sleep in their kennel and gone out to seek for the pipit's nest? Have fox and armadillo met to challenge each other to fresh trials of strength and cunning? What is the owl saying this moment to his mistress in praise of her big green eyes?"

The young man smiled slightly but answered not; and for full five minutes more all listened, then sounds of approaching hoofs became audible. Dogs began to bark, horses to snort in alarm, and Gregory rose and went forth to receive the late night-wanderer.

Soon he appeared, beating the angry barking dogs off with his whip, a white-faced, wild-haired man, furiously spurring his horse like a person demented or flying from robbers.

"Ave Maria!" he shouted aloud; and when the answer was given in suitable pious words, the scared-looking stranger drew near, and bending down said, "Tell me, good friend, is one whom men call Niño Diablo with you; for to this house I have been directed in my search for him?"

"He is within, friend," answered Gregory. "Follow me and you shall see him with your own eyes. Only first unsaddle, so that your horse may roll before the sweat dries on him."

"How many horses have I ridden their last journey on this quest!" said the stranger, hurriedly pulling off the saddle and rugs. "But tell me one thing more: is he well—no indisposition? Has he met with no accident—a broken bone, a sprained ankle?"

"Friend," said Gregory, "I have heard that once in past times the moon met with an accident, but of the Niño no such thing has been reported to me."

With this assurance the stranger followed

his host into the kitchen, made his salutation, and sat down by the fire. He was about thirty years old, a good-looking man, but his face was haggard, his eyes bloodshot, his manner restless, and he appeared like one half-crazed by some great calamity. The hospitable Magdalen placed food before him and pressed him to eat. He complied, although reluctantly, despatched his supper in a few moments, and murmured a prayer; then, glancing curiously at the two men seated near him, he addressed himself to the burly, well-armed, and dangerous-looking Polycarp. "Friend," he said, his agitation increasing as he spoke, "four days have I been seeking you, taking neither food nor rest, so great was my need of your assistance. You alone, after God, can help me. Help me in this strait, and half of all I possess in land and cattle and gold shall be freely given to you, and the angels above will applaud your deed!"

"Drunk or mad?" was the only reply vouchsafed to this appeal.

"Sir," said the stranger with dignity, "I have not tasted wine these many days, nor has my great grief crazed me."

"Then what ails the man?" said Polycarp.

"Fear perhaps, for he is white in the face like one who has seen the Indians."

"In truth I have seen them. I was one of those unfortunates who first opposed them, and most of the friends who were with me are now food for wild dogs. Where our houses stood there are only ashes and a stain of blood on the ground. Oh, friend, can you not guess why you alone were in my thoughts when this trouble came to me—why I have ridden day and night to find you?"

"Demons!" exclaimed Polycarp, "into what quagmires would this man lead me? Once for all I understand you not! Leave me in peace, strange man, or we shall quarrel." And here he tapped his weapon significantly.

At this juncture, Gregory, who took his time about everything, thought proper to interpose. "You are mistaken, friend," said he. "The young man sitting on your right is the Niño Diablo, for whom you inquired a little while ago."

A look of astonishment, followed by one of intense relief, came over the stranger's face. Turning to the young man he said, "My friend, forgive me this mistake. Grief has perhaps dimmed my sight; but sometimes the iron blade and the blade of finest temper are not easily distinguished by the eye. When we try them we know which is the brute metal, and cast it aside to take up the other, and trust our life to it. The words I have spoken were meant for you, and you have heard them."

"What can I do for you, friend?" said the Niño.

"Oh, sir, the greatest service! You can restore my lost wife to me. The savages have taken her away into captivity. What can I do to save her—I who cannot make myself invisible, and fly like the wind, and compass all things!" And here he bowed his head, and covering his face gave way to over-mastering grief.

"Be comforted, friend," said the other, touching him lightly on the arm. "I will restore her to you."

"Oh, friend, how shall I thank you for these words!" cried the unhappy man, seizing and pressing the Niño's hand.

"Tell me her name—describe her to me."

"Torcuata is her name—Torcuata de la Rosa. She is one finger's width taller than this young woman," indicating one of the twins who was standing. "But not dark; her cheeks

are rosy—no, no, I forget, they will be pale
now, whiter than the grass plumes, with stains
of dark colour under the eyes.   Brown hair
and blue eyes, but very deep blue.   Look well,
friend, lest you think them black and leave her
to perish."

"Never!" remarked Gregory, shaking his
head.

"Enough—you have told me enough,
friend," said the Niño, rolling up a cigarette.

"Enough!" repeated the other, surprised.
"But you do not know; she is my life; my
life is in your hands.   How can I persuade
you to be with me?   Cattle I have.   I had
gone to pay the herdsmen their wages when
the Indians came unexpectedly; and my house
at La Chilca, on the banks of the Langueyú,
was burnt, and my wife taken away during my
absence.   Eight hundred head of cattle have
escaped the savages, and half of them shall be
yours; and half of all I possess in money and
land."

"Cattle!" returned the Niño, smiling, and
holding a lighted stick to his cigarette.   "I
have enough to eat without molesting myself
with the care of cattle."

"But I told you that I had other things," said the stranger, full of distress.

The young man laughed, and rose from his seat.

"Listen to me," he said. "I go now to follow the Indians—to mix with them, perhaps. They are retreating slowly, burdened with much spoil. In fifteen days go to the little town of Tandil, and wait for me there. As for land, if God has given so much of it to the ostrich it is not a thing for a man to set a great value on." Then he bent down to whisper a few words in the ear of the girl at his side; and immediately afterwards, with a simple "good-night" to the others, stepped lightly from the kitchen. By another door the girl also hurriedly left the room, to hide her tears from the watchful censuring eyes of mother and aunt.

Then the stranger, recovering from his astonishment at the abrupt ending of the conversation, started up, and crying aloud, "Stay! stay one moment—one word more!" rushed out after the young man. At some distance from the house he caught sight of the Niño, sitting motionless on his horse, as if waiting to speak to him.

"This is what I have to say to you," spoke the Niño, bending down to the other. "Go back to Langueyú, and rebuild your house, and expect me there with your wife in about thirty days. When I bade you go to the Tandil in fifteen days, I spoke only to mislead that man Polycarp, who has an evil mind. Can I ride a hundred leagues and back in fifteen days? Say no word of this to any man. And fear not. If I fail to return with your wife at the appointed time take some of that money you have offered me, and bid a priest say a mass for my soul's repose; for eye of man shall never see me again, and the brown hawks will be complaining that there is no more flesh to be picked from my bones."

During this brief colloquy, and afterwards, when Gregory and his women-folk went off to bed, leaving the stranger to sleep in his rugs beside the kitchen fire, Polycarp, who had sworn a mighty oath not to close his eyes that night, busied himself making his horses secure. Driving them home, he tied them to the posts of the gate within twenty-five yards of the kitchen door. Then he sat down by the fire and smoked and dozed, and cursed his dry mouth and drowsy eyes that were so hard to keep open. At intervals of about fifteen minutes he would get up and go out to satisfy himself that his precious horses were still safe. At length in rising, some time after midnight, his foot kicked against some loud-sounding metal object lying beside him on the floor, which on examination, proved to be a copper bell of a peculiar shape, and curiously like the one fastened to the neck of his bell-mare. Bell in hand, he stepped to the door and put out his head, and lo! his horses were no longer at the gate! Eight horses: seven iron-grey geldings, every one of them swift and sure-footed, sound as the bell in his hand, and as like each other as seven claret-coloured eggs in the tinamou's nest; and the eighth the gentle piebald mare—the *madrina* his horses loved and would follow to the world's end, now, alas! with a thief on her back! Gone—gone!

He rushed out, uttering a succession of frantic howls and imprecations; and finally, to wind up the performance, dashed the now useless bell with all his energy against the gate, shattering it into a hundred pieces. Oh, that bell, how often and how often in how many a wayside public-house had he boasted, in his cups and when sober, of its mellow, far-reaching tone,—the sweet sound that assured him in the silent watches of the night that his beloved steeds were safe! Now he danced on the broken fragments, digging them into the earth with his heel; now in his frenzy, he could have dug them up again to grind them to powder with his teeth!

The children turned restlessly in bed, dreaming of the lost little girl in the desert; and the stranger half awoke, muttering, "Courage, O Torcuata—let not your heart break. . . . Soul of my life, he gives you back to me—on my bosom, *rosa fresca, rosa fresca!*" Then the hands unclenched themselves again, and the muttering died away. But Gregory woke fully, and instantly divined the cause of the clamour. "Magdalen! Wife!" he said. "Listen to Polycarp; the Niño has paid him out for his insolence! Oh, fool, I warned him, and he would not listen!" But Magdalen refused to wake; and so, hiding his head under the coverlet, he made the bed shake with suppressed laughter, so pleased was he at the clever trick played on his blustering cousin. All at once his laughter ceased, and out popped his head again, showing in the

dim light a somewhat long and solemn face.
For he had suddenly thought of his pretty
daughter asleep in the adjoining room.
Asleep! Wide awake, more likely, thinking
of her sweet lover, brushing the dews from the
hoary pampas grass in his southward flight,
speeding away into the heart of the vast mysterious wilderness. Listening also to her
uncle, the desperado, apostrophizing the midnight stars; while with his knife he excavates
two deep trenches, three yards long and inter-
secting each other at right angles—a sacred
symbol on which he intends, when finished, to
swear a most horrible vengeance. "Perhaps,"
muttered Gregory, "the Niño has still other
pranks to play in this house."

When the stranger heard next morning what
had happened, he was better able to understand the Niño's motive in giving him that
caution overnight; nor was he greatly put out,
but thought it better that an evil-minded man
should lose his horses than that the Niño
should set out badly mounted on such an ad-
venture.

"Let me not forget," said the robbed man,
as he rode away on a horse borrowed from his
cousin, "to be at the Tandil this day fortnight,

with a sharp knife and a blunderbuss charged
with a handful of powder and not fewer than
twenty-three slugs."

Terribly in earnest was Polycarp of the
South! He was there at the appointed time,
slugs and all; but the smooth-cheeked, mysterious, child-devil came not; nor, stranger still,
did the scared-looking de la Rosa come clatter-
ing in to look for his lost Torcuata. At the
end of the fifteenth day de la Rosa was at
Langueyú, seventy-five miles from the Tandil,
alone in his new rancho, which had just been
rebuilt with the aid of a few neighbours.
Through all that night he sat alone by the fire,
pondering many things. If he could only recover his lost wife, then he would bid a long
farewell to that wild frontier and take her
across the great sea, and to that old tree-shaded
stone farm-house in Andalusia, which he had
left a boy, and where his aged parents still
lived, thinking no more to see their wandering
son. His resolution was taken; he would sell
all he possessed, all except a portion of land
in the Langueyú with the house he had just
rebuilt; and to the Niño Diablo, the deliverer,
he would say, "Friend, though you despise the
things that others value, take this land and

poor house for the sake of the girl Magdalen you love; for then perhaps her parents will no longer deny her to you."

He was still thinking of these things, when a dozen or twenty military starlings—that cheerful scarlet-breasted songster of the lonely pampas—alighted on the thatch outside, and warbling their gay, careless winter-music told him that it was day. And all day long, on foot and on horseback, his thoughts were of his lost Torcuata; and when evening once more drew near his heart was sick with suspense and longing; and climbing the ladder placed against the gable of his rancho he stood on the roof gazing westwards into the blue distance. The sun, crimson and large, sunk into the great green sea of grass, and from all the plain rose the tender fluting notes of the tinamou-partridges, bird answering bird. "Oh, that I could pierce the haze with my vision," he murmured, "that I could see across a hundred leagues of level plain, and look this moment on your sweet face, Torcuata!"

And Torcuata was in truth a hundred leagues distant from him at that moment; and if the miraculous sight he wished for had been given, this was what he would have seen: A wide barren plain scantily clothed with yellow tufts of grass and thorny shrubs, and at its southern extremity, shutting out the view on that side, a low range of dune-like hills. Over this level ground, towards the range, moves a vast herd of cattle and horses—fifteen or twenty thousand head—followed by a scattered horde of savages armed with their long lances. In a small compact body in the centre ride the captives, women and children. Just as the red orb touches the horizon the hills are passed, and lo! a wide grassy valley beyond, with flocks and herds pasturing, and scattered trees, and the blue gleam of water from a chain of small lakes! There full in sight, is the Indian settlement, the smoke rising peacefully up from the clustered huts. At the sight of home the savages burst into loud cries of joy and triumph, answered, as they drew near, with piercing screams of welcome from the village population, chiefly composed of women, children and old men.

It is past midnight; the young moon has set; the last fires are dying down; the shouts and loud noise of excited talk and laughter have ceased, and the weary warriors, after feasting on sweet mare's flesh to repletion, have fallen asleep in their huts, or lying out of doors on the ground. Only the dogs are excited still and keep up an incessant barking. Even the captive women, huddled together in one hut in the middle of the settlement, fatigued with their long rough journey, have cried themselves to sleep at last.

At length one of the sad sleepers wakes, or half wakes, dreaming that some one has called her name. How could such a thing be? Yet her own name still seems ringing in her brain, and at length, fully awake, she finds herself intently listening. Again it sounded—"Torcuata"—a voice fine as the pipe of a mosquito, yet so sharp and distinct that it tingled in her ear. She sat up and listened again, and once more it sounded "Torcuata!" "Who speaks?" she returned in a fearful whisper. The voice, still fine and small, replied, "Come out from among the others until you touch the wall." Trembling she obeyed, creeping out from among the sleepers until she came into contact with the side of the hut. Then the voice sounded again, "Creep round the wall until you come to a small crack of light on the other side." Again she obeyed, and when she reached the line of faint light it widened quickly to an aperture, through which a shadowy arm was passed round her waist; and in a moment she was lifted up, and saw the stars above her, and at her feet dark forms of men wrapped in their ponchos lying asleep. But no one woke, no alarm was given; and in a very few minutes she was mounted, man-fashion, on a bare-backed horse, speeding swiftly over the dim plains, with a shadowy form of her mysterious deliverer some yards in advance, driving before him a score or so of horses. He had only spoken half-a-dozen words to her since their escape from the hut, but she knew by those words that he was taking her to Langueyú.

MARTA RIQUELME

MARTA RIQUELME

(From the Sepulvida MSS.)

I

FAR away from the paths of those who wander to and fro on the earth, sleeps Jujuy in the heart of this continent. It is the remotest of our provinces, and divided from the countries of the Pacific by the giant range of the Cordillera; a region of mountains and forest, torrid heats and great storms; and although in itself a country half as large as the Spanish peninsula, it possesses, as its only means of communication with the outside world, a few insignificant roads which are scarcely more than mule-paths.

The people of this region have few wants; they aspire not after progress, and have never changed their ancient manner of life. The Spanish were long in conquering them: and now, after three centuries of Christian dominion, they still speak the Quichua, and subsist in a great measure on patay, a sweet paste made from the pod of the wild algarroba tree; while they still retain as a beast of burden the llama, a gift of their old masters the Peruvian Incas.

This much is common knowledge, but of the peculiar character of the country, or of the nature of the things which happen within its borders, nothing is known to those without; Jujuy being to them only a country lying over against the Andes, far removed from and unaffected by the progress of the world. It has pleased Providence to give me a more intimate knowledge, and this has been a sore affliction and great burden now for many years. But I have not taken up my pen to complain that all the years of my life are consumed in a region where the great spiritual enemy of mankind is still permitted to challenge the supremacy of our Master, waging an equal war against his followers: my sole object is to warn, perhaps also to comfort, others who will be my successors in this place, and who will come to the church of Yala ignorant of the means which will be used for the destruction of their souls. And if I set down anything in this narrative which might be injurious to our holy religion, owing to the darkness of our understandings and the little faith that is in us, I pray that the sin I now ignorantly commit may be forgiven me, and that this manuscript may perish miraculously unread by any person.

I was educated for the priesthood, in the city of Cordova, that famous seminary of learning and religion; and in 1838, being then in my twenty-seventh year, I was appointed priest to a small settlement in the distant province of which I have spoken. The habit of obedience, early instilled in me by my Jesuit masters, enabled me to accept this command unmurmuringly, and even with an outward show of cheerfulness. Nevertheless it filled me with grief, although I might have suspected that some such hard fate had been designed for me, since I had been made to study the Quichua language, which is now only spoken in the Andean provinces. With secret bitter repinings I tore myself from all that made life pleasant and desirable—the society of innumerable friends, the libraries, the beautiful church where I had worshipped, and that renowned University which has shed on the troubled annals of our unhappy country whatever lustre of learning and poetry they possess.

My first impressions of Jujuy did not serve to raise my spirits. After a trying journey of four weeks' duration—the roads being difficult and the country greatly disturbed at the time—I reached the capital of the province, also called Jujuy, a town of about two thousand inhabitants. Thence I journeyed to my destination, a settlement called Yala, situated on the northwestern border of the province, where the river Yala takes its rise, at the foot of that range of mountains which, branching eastwards from the Andes, divides Jujuy from Bolivia. I was wholly unprepared for the character of the place I had come to live in. Yala was a scattered village of about ninety souls—ignorant, apathetic people, chiefly Indians. To my unaccustomed sight the country appeared a rude, desolate chaos of rocks and gigantic mountains, compared with which the famous sierras of Cordova sunk into mere hillocks, and of vast gloomy forests, whose death-like stillness was broken only by the savage screams of some strange fowl, or by the hoarse thunders of a distant waterfall.

As soon as I had made myself known to the

people of the village, I set myself to acquire a knowledge of the surrounding country; but before long I began to despair of ever finding the limits of my parish in any direction. The country was wild, being only tenanted by a few widely-separated families, and like all deserts it was distasteful to me in an eminent degree; but as I would frequently be called upon to perform long journeys, I resolved to learn as much as possible of its geography. Always striving to overcome my own inclinations, which made a studious, sedentary life most congenial, I aimed at being very active; and having procured a good mule I began taking long rides every day, without a guide and with only a pocket compass to prevent me from losing myself. I could never altogether overcome my natural aversion to silent deserts, and in my long rides I avoided the thick forest and deep valleys, keeping as much as possible to the open plain.

One day having ridden about twelve or fourteen miles from Yala, I discovered a tree of noble proportions growing by itself in the open, and feeling much oppressed by the heat I alighted from my mule and stretched myself on the ground under the grateful shade.

There was a continuous murmur of leche-guanas—a small honey wasp—in the foliage above me, for the tree was in flower, and this soothing sound soon brought that restful feeling to my mind which insensibly leads to slumber. I was, however, still far from sleep, but reclining with eyes half closed, thinking of nothing, when suddenly, from the depths of the dense leafage above me, rang forth a shriek, the most terrible it has ever fallen to the lot of any human being to hear. In sound it was a human cry, yet expressing a degree of agony and despair surpassing the power of any human soul to feel, and my impression was that it could only have been uttered by some tortured spirit allowed to wander for a season on the earth. Shriek after shriek, each more powerful and terrible to hear than the last, succeeded, and I sprang to my feet, the hair standing erect on my head, a profuse sweat of terror breaking out all over me. The cause of all these maddening sounds remained invisible to my eyes; and finally running to my mule I climbed hastily on to its back and never ceased flogging the poor beast all the way back to Yala.

On reaching my house I sent for one Osuna,

a man of substance, able to converse in
Spanish, and much respected in the village.
In the evening he came to see me, and I then
gave an account of the extraordinary experience I had encountered that day.

"Do not distress yourself, Father—you have
only heard the Kakué," he replied. I then
learnt from him that the Kakué is a fowl fre-
quenting the most gloomy and sequestered
forests and known to every one in the country
for its terrible voice. Kakué, he also informed me, was the ancient name of the country, but the word was misspelt Jujuy by the
early explorers, and this corrupted name was
eventually retained. All this, which I now
heard for the first time, is historical; but when
he proceeded to inform me that the Kakué is
a metamorphosed human being, that women
and sometimes men, whose lives have been
darkened with great suffering and calamities,
are changed by compassionate spirits into
these lugubrious birds, I asked him somewhat
contemptuously whether he, an enlightened
man, believed a thing so absurd.

"There is not in all Jujuy," he replied, "a
person who disbelieves it."

"That is a mere assertion," cried I, "but it

shows which way your mind inclines. No doubt the superstition concerning the Kakué is very ancient, and has come down to us together with the Quichua language from the aborigines. Transformations of men into animals are common in all the primitive religions of South America. Thus, the Guaranies relate that flying from a conflagration caused by the descent of the sun to the earth many people cast themselves into the river Paraguay, and were incontinently changed into capybaras and caymans; while others who took refuge in trees were blackened and scorched by the heat and became monkeys. But to go no further than the traditions of the Incas who once ruled over this region, it is related that after the first creation the entire human family, inhabiting the slopes of the Andes, were changed into crickets by a demon at enmity with man's first creator. Throughout the continent these ancient beliefs are at present either dead or dying out; and if the Kakué legend still maintains its hold on the vulgar here it is owing to the isolated position of the country, hemmed in by vast mountains and having no intercouse with neighbouring states."

Perceiving that my arguments had entirely failed to produce any effect I began to lose my temper, and demanded whether he, a Christian, dared to profess belief in a fable born of the corrupt imagination of the heathen?

He shrugged his shoulders and replied, "I have only stated what we, in Jujuy, know to be a fact. What is, is; and if you talk until to-morrow you cannot make it different, although you may prove yourself a very learned person."

His answer produced a strange effect on me. For the first time in my life I experienced the sensation of anger in all its power. Rising to my feet I paced the floor excitedly, and using many gestures, smiting the table with my hands and shaking my clenched fist close to his face in a threatening manner, and with a violence of language unbecoming in a follower of Christ, I denounced the degrading ignorance and heathenish condition of mind of the people I had come to live with; and more particularly of the person before me, who had some pretensions to education and should have been free from the gross delusions of the vulgar. While addressing him in this tone he sat smoking a cigarette, blowing rings from his lips and placidly watching them rise towards the ceiling, and with his studied supercilious indifference aggravated my rage to such a degree that I could scarcely restrain myself from flying at his throat or striking him to the earth with one of the cane-bottomed chairs in the room.

As soon as he left me, however, I was overwhelmed with remorse at having behaved in a manner so unseemly. I spent the night in penitent tears and prayers, and resolved in future to keep a strict watch over myself, now that the secret enemy of my soul had revealed itself to me. Nor did I make this resolution a moment too soon. I had hitherto regarded myself as a person of a somewhat mild and placid disposition; the sudden change to new influences, and, perhaps also, the secret disgust I felt at my lot, had quickly developed my true character, which now became impatient to a degree and prone to sudden violent outbursts of passion during which I had little control over my tongue. The perpetual watch over myself and struggle against my evil nature which had now become necessary was the cause of but half my trouble. I discovered that my parishioners, with scarcely an exception, possessed that dull apathetic temper of mind concerning spiritual things, which had so greatly exasperated me in the man Osuna, and which obstructed all my efforts to benefit them. These people, or rather their ancestors centuries ago, had accepted Christianity, but it had never properly filtered down into their hearts. It was on the surface still; and if their half-heathen minds were deeply stirred it was not by the story of the Passion of our Lord, but by some superstitious belief inherited from their progenitors. During all the years I have spent in Yala I never said a Mass, never preached a sermon, never attempted to speak of the consolations of faith, without having the thought thrust on to me that my words were useless, that I was watering the rock where no seed could germinate, and wasting my life in vain efforts to impart religion to souls that were proof against it. Often have I been reminded of our holy and learned Father Guevara's words, when he complains of the difficulties encountered by the earlier Jesuit missionaries. He relates how he endeavoured to impress the Chiriguanos with the danger they incurred by refusing baptism, picturing to them their future

condition when they would be condemned to
everlasting fire.   To which they only replied
that they were not disturbed by what he told
them, but were, on the contrary, greatly
pleased to hear that the flames of the future
would be unquenchable, for that would save
them infinite trouble, and if they found the
fire too hot they would remove themselves to
a proper distance from it.   So hard it was
for their heathen intellects to comprehend the
solemn doctrines of our faith!

II

MY knowledge of the Quichua language, acquired solely by the study of the vocabularies, was at first of little advantage to me. I found myself unable to converse on familiar topics with the people of Yala; and this was a great difficulty in my way, and a cause of distress for more reasons than one. I was unprovided with books, or other means of profit and recreation, and therefore eagerly sought out the few people in the place able to converse in Spanish, for I have always been fond of social intercourse. There were only four: one very old man, who died shortly after my arrival; another was Osuna, a man for whom I had conceived an unconquerable aversion; the other two were women, the widow Riquelme and her daughter. About this girl I must speak at some length, since it is with her fortunes that this narrative is chiefly concerned. The widow Riquelme was poor, having only a house in Yala, but with a garden sufficiently large to

grow a plentiful provision of fruit and vege-
tables, and to feed a few goats, so that these
women had enough to live on, without osten-
tation, from their plot of ground. They were
of pure Spanish blood; the mother was pre-
maturely old and faded; Marta, who was a
little over fifteen when I arrived at Yala, was
the loveliest being I had ever beheld; though
in this matter my opinion may be biassed, for
I only saw her side by side with the dark-
skinned coarse-haired Indian women, and
compared with their faces of ignoble type
Marta's was like that of an angel. Her
features were regular; her skin white, but with
that pale darkness in it seen in some whose
families have lived for generations in tropical
countries. Her eyes, shaded by long lashes,
were of that violet tint seen sometimes in
people of Spanish blood—eyes which appear
black until looked at closely. Her hair was,
however, the crown of her beauty and chief
glory, for it was of great length and a dark
shining gold colour—a thing wonderful to
see!

The society of these two women, who were
full of sympathy and sweetness, promised to be
a great boon to me, and I was often with them;

but very soon I discovered that, on the contrary, it was only about to add a fresh bitterness to my existence. The Christian affection I felt for this beautiful child insensibly degenerated into a mundane passion of such overmastering strength that all my efforts to pluck it out of my heart proved ineffectual. I cannot describe my unhappy condition during the long months when I vainly wrestled with this sinful emotion, and when I often thought in the bitterness of my heart that my God had forsaken me. The fear that the time would come when my feelings would betray themselves increased on me until at length, to avoid so great an evil, I was compelled to cease visiting the only house in Yala where it was a pleasure for me to enter. What had I done to be thus cruelly persecuted by Satan? was the constant cry of my soul. Now I know that this temptation was only a part of that long and desperate struggle in which the servants of the prince of the power of the air had engaged to overthrow me.

Not for five years did this conflict with myself cease to be a constant danger—a period which seemed to my mind not less than half a century. Nevertheless, knowing that idleness is the parent of evil, I was incessantly occupied; for when there was nothing to call me abroad, I laboured with my pen at home, filling in this way from volumes, which in the end may serve to throw some light on the great historical question of the Incas' Cis-Andean dominion, and its effect on the conquered nations.

When Marta was twenty years old it became known in Yala that she had promised her hand in marriage to one Cosme Luna, and of this person a few words must be said. Like many young men, possessing no property or occupation, and having no disposition to work, he was a confirmed gambler, spending all his time going about from town to town to attend horse-races and cock-fights. I had for a long time regarded him as an abominable pest in Yala, a wretch possessing a hundred vices under a pleasing exterior, and not one redeeming virtue, and it was therefore with the deepest pain that I heard of his success with Marta. The widow, who was naturally disappointed at her daughter's choice, came to me with tears and complaints, begging me to assist her in persuading her beloved child to break off an engagement which promised only to make her unhappy for life. But with that secret feeling in my heart, ever-striving to drag me down to my ruin, I dared not help her, albeit, I would gladly have given my right hand to save Marta from the calamity of marrying such a man.

The tempest which these tidings had raised in my heart never abated while the preparations for the marriage were going on. I was forced now to abandon my work, for I was incapable of thought; nor did all my religious exercises avail to banish for one moment the strange, sullen rage which had taken complete possession of me. Night after night I would rise from my bed and pace the floor of my room for hours, vainly trying to shut out the promptings of some fiend perpetually urging me to take some desperate course against this young man. A thousand schemes for his destruction suggested themselves to my mind, and when I had resolutely dismissed them all and prayed that my sinful temper might be forgiven, I would rise from my knees still cursing him a thousand times more than ever.

In the meantime, Marta herself saw nothing wrong in Cosme, for love had blinded her. He was young, good looking, could play on the guitar and sing, and was master of that easy, playful tone in conversation which is always pleasing to women. Moreover, he dressed well and was generous with his money, with which he was apparently well provided.

In due time they were married, and Cosme, having no house of his own, came to live with his mother-in-law in Yala. Then, at length, what I had foreseen also happened. He ran out of money, and his new relations had nothing he could lay his hands on to sell. He was too proud to gamble for coppers, and the poor people of Yala had no silver to risk; he could not or would not work, and the vacant life he was living began to grow wearisome. Once more he took to his old courses, and it soon grew to be a common thing for him to be absent from home for a month or six weeks at a time. Marta looked unhappy, but would not complain or listen to a word against Cosme; for whenever he returned to Yala then his wife's great beauty was like a new thing to him, bringing him to her feet, and making him again for a brief season her devoted lover and slave.

She at length became a mother. For her sake I was glad; for now with her infant boy to occupy her mind Cosme's neglect would seem more endurable. He was away when the child was born; he had gone, it was reported, into Catamarca, and for three months nothing was heard of him. This was a season of political troubles, and men being required to recruit the forces, all persons found wandering about the country not engaged in any lawful occupation, were taken for military service. And this had happened to Cosme. A letter from him reached Marta at last, informing her that he had been carried away to San Luis, and asking her to send him two hundred pesos, as with that amount he would be able to purchase his release. But it was impossible for her to raise the money; nor could she leave Yala to go to him, for her mother's strength was now rapidly failing, and Marta could not abandon her to the care of strangers. All this she was obliged to tell Cosme in the letter she wrote to him, and which perhaps never reached his hands, for no reply to it ever came.

At length, the widow Riquelme died; then Marta sold the house and garden and all she possessed, and taking her child with her, went out to seek her husband. Travelling first to the town of Jujuy, she there, with other women, attached herself to a convoy about to start on a journey to the southern provinces. Several months went by, and then came the disastrous tidings to Yala that the convoy had been surprised by Indians in a lonely place and all the people slain.

I will not here dwell on the anguish of mind I endured on learning Marta's sad end: for I tried hard to believe that her troubled life was indeed over, although I was often assured by my neighbours that the Indians invariably spare the women and children.

Every blow dealt by a cruel destiny against this most unhappy woman had pierced my heart; and during the years that followed, and when the villagers had long ceased to speak of her, often in the dead of the night I rose and sought the house where she had lived, and walking under the trees in that garden where I had so often held intercourse with her, indulged a grief which time seemed powerless to mitigate.

III

MARTA was not dead; but what happened to her after her departure from Yala was this. When the convoy with which she journeyed was attacked the men only were slain, while the women and children were carried away into captivity. When the victors divided the spoil among themselves, the child, which even in that long painful journey into the desert, with the prospect of a life of cruel slavery before her, had been a comfort to Marta, was taken forcibly from her arms to be conveyed to some distant place, and from that moment she utterly lost sight of it. She herself was bought by an Indian able to pay for a pretty white captive, and who presently made her his wife. She, a Christian, the wife of a man loved only too well, could not endure this horrible fate which had overtaken her. She was also mad with grief at the loss of her child, and stealing out one dark stormy night she fled from the Indian settlement. For several days and nights she wandered about the desert, suffering every hardship and in constant fear of jaguars, and was at length found by the savages in a half-starved condition and unable longer to fly from them. Her owner, when she was restored to him, had no mercy on her: he bound her to a tree growing beside his hovel, and there every day he cruelly scourged her naked flesh to satisfy his barbarous resentment, until she was ready to perish with excessive suffering. He also cut off her hair, and braiding it into a belt wore it always round his waist,—a golden trophy which doubtless won him great honour and distinction amongst his fellow savages. When he had by these means utterly broken her spirit and reduced her to the last condition of weakness, he released her from the tree, but at the same time fastened a log of wood to her ankle, so that only with great labour, and drawing herself along with the aid of her hands, could she perform the daily tasks her master imposed on her. Only after a whole year of captivity, and when she had given birth to a child, was the punishment over and her foot released from the log. The natural affection which she felt for this child of a father so cruel was now poor Marta's only comfort. In this hard servitude five years of her miserable existence were consumed; and only those who know the stern, sullen, pitiless character of the Indian can imagine what this period was for Marta, without sympathy from her fellow-creatures, with no hope and no pleasure beyond the pleasure of loving and caressing her own infant savages. Of these she was now the mother of three.

When her youngest was not many months old Marta had one day wandered some distance in search of sticks for firewood, when a woman, one of her fellow-captives from Jujuy, came running to her, for she had been watching for an opportunity of speaking with Marta. It happened that this woman had succeeded in persuading her Indian husband to take her back to her home in the Christian country, and she had at the same time won his consent to take Marta with them, having conceived a great affection for her. The prospect of escape filled poor Marta's heart with joy, but when she was told that her children could on no account be taken, then a cruel struggle commenced in her breast. Bitterly she pleaded for permission to take her babes, and at last, overcome by her importunity, her

fellow-captive consented to her taking the
youngest of the three; though this concession
was made very reluctantly.

In a short time the day appointed for the
flight arrived, and Marta carrying her infant
met her friends in the wood. They were
quickly mounted, and the journey began which
was to last for many days, and during which
they were to suffer much from hunger, thirst
and fatigue. One dark night as they
journeyed through a hilly and wooded country, Marta being overcome with fatigue so that
she could scarcely keep her seat, the Indian
with affected kindness relieved her of the child
she always carried in her arms. An hour
passed, and then pressing forward to his side
and asking for her child she was told that it
had been dropped into a deep, swift stream
over which they had swam their horses some
time before. Of what happened after that she
was unable to give any very clear account.
She only dimly remembered that through
many days of scorching heat and many nights
of weary travel she was always piteously
pleading for her lost child—always seeming to
hear it crying to her to save it from destruction. The long journey ended at last. She

was left by the others at the first Christian settlement they reached, after which travelling slowly from village to village she made her way to Yala. Her old neighbours and friends did not know her at first, but when they were at length convinced that it was indeed Marta Riquelme that stood before them she was welcomed like one returned from the grave. I heard of her arrival, and hastening forth to greet her found her seated before a neighbour's house already surrounded by half the people of the village.

Was this woman indeed Marta, once the pride of Yala! It was hard to believe it, so darkened with the burning suns and winds of years was her face, once so fair; so wasted and furrowed with grief and the many hardships she had undergone! Her figure, worn almost to a skeleton, was clothed with ragged garments, while her head, bowed down with sorrow and despair, was divested of that golden crown which had been her chief ornament. Seeing me arrive she cast herself on her knees before me and taking my hand in hers covered it with tears and kisses. The grief I felt at the sight of her forlorn condition mingled with joy for her deliverance from death and captivity overcame me; I was shaken like a reed in the wind, and covering my face with my robe I sobbed aloud in the presence of all the people.

IV

EVERYTHING that charity could dictate was done to alleviate her misery. A merciful woman of Yala received her into her house and provided her with decent garments. But for a time nothing served to raise her desponding spirits; she still grieved for her lost babe, and seemed ever in fancy listening to its piteous cries for help. When assured that Cosme would return in due time that alone gave her comfort. She believed what they told her, for it agreed with her wish, and by degrees the effects of her terrible experience began to wear off, giving place to a feeling of feverish impatience with which she looked forward to her husband's return. With this feeling, which I did all I could to encourage, perceiving it to be the only remedy against despair, came also a new anxiety about her personal appearance. She grew careful in her dress, and made the most of her short and sunburnt hair. Beauty she could never recover; but she possessed good features which

could not be altered; her eyes also retained
their violet colour, and hope brought back to
her something of the vanished expression of
other years.

At length, when she had been with us over a
year, one day there came a report that Cosme
had arrived, that he had been seen in Yala, and
had alighted at Andrada's door—the store in
the main road.   She heard it and rose up with
a great cry of joy.   He had come to her at
last—he would comfort her!   She could not
wait for his arrival: what wonder!   Hurrying forth she flew like the wind through the
village, and in a few moments stood on Andrada's threshold, panting from her race, her
cheeks glowing, all the hope and life and fire
of her girlhood rushing back to her heart.
There she beheld Cosme, changed but little,
surrounded by his old companions, listening
in silence and with a dismayed countenance to
the story of Marta's sufferings in the great
desert, of her escape and return to Yala, where
she had been received like one come back from
the sepulchre.   Presently they caught sight
of her standing there.   "Here is Marta herself arrived in good time," they cried.   "Behold your wife!"

He shook himself from them with a strange laugh. "What, that woman my wife—Marta Riquelme!" he replied. "No, no, my friends, be not deceived; Marta perished long ago in the desert, where I have been to seek for her. Of her death I have no doubt; let me pass."

He pushed by her, left her standing there motionless as a statue, unable to utter a word, and was quickly on his horse riding away from Yala.

Then suddenly she recovered possession of her faculties, and with a cry of anguish hurried after him, imploring him to return to her; but finding that he would not listen to her she was overcome with despair and fell upon the earth insensible. She was taken up by the people who had followed her out and carried back into the house. Unhappily she was not dead, and when she recovered consciousness it was pitiful to hear the excuses she invented for the remorseless wretch who had abandoned her. She was altered, she said, greatly altered —it was not strange that Cosme had refused to believe that she could be the Marta of six years ago! In her heart she knew that no- body was deceived: to all Yala it was patent that she had been deserted. She could not endure it, and when she met people in the street she lowered her eyes and passed on, pretending not to see them. Most of her time was spent indoors, and there she would sit for hours without speaking or stirring, her cheeks resting on her hands, her eyes fixed on vacancy. My heart bled for her; morning and evening I remembered her in my prayers; by every argument I sought to cheer her drooping spirit, even telling her that the beauty and freshness of her youth would return to her in time, and that her husband would repent and come back to her.

These efforts were fruitless. Before many days she disappeared from Yala, and though diligent search was made in the adjacent mountains she could not be found. Knowing how empty and desolate her life had been, deprived of every object of affection, I formed the opinion that she had gone back to the desert to seek the tribe where she had been a captive in the hope of once more seeing her lost children. At length, when all expectation of ever seeing her again had been abandoned, a person named Montero came to me with tidings of her. He was a poor man, a charcoal-burner, and lived with his wife and children in the forest about two hours' journey from Yala, at a distance from any other habitation. Finding Marta wandering lost in the woods he had taken her to his rancho, and she had been pleased to find this shelter, away from the people of Yala who knew her history; and it was at Marta's own request that this good man had ridden to the village to inform me of her safety. I was greatly relieved to hear all this, and thought that Marta had acted wisely in escaping from the villagers, who were always pointing her out and repeating her wonderful history. In that sequestered spot where she had taken refuge, removed from sad associations and gossiping tongues, the wounds in her heart would perhaps gradually heal and peace return to her perturbed spirit.

Before many weeks had elapsed, however, Montero's wife came to me with a very sad account of Marta. She had grown day by day more silent and solitary in her habits, spending most of her time in some secluded spot among the trees, where she would sit motionless, brooding over her memories for hours at a time. Nor was this the worst. Occasionally she would make an effort to assist in the household work, preparing the patay or maize for the supper, or going out with Montero's wife to gather firewood in the forest. But suddenly, in the middle of her task, she would drop her bundle of sticks and, casting herself on the earth, break forth into the most heart-rending cries and lamentations, loudly exclaiming that God had unjustly persecuted her, that He was a being filled with malevolence, and speaking many things against Him very dreadful to hear. Deeply distressed at these tidings I called for my mule and accompanied the poor woman back to her own house; but when we arrived there Marta could nowhere be found.

Most willingly would I have remained to see her, and try once more to win her back from these desponding moods, but I was compelled to return to Yala. For it happened that a fever epidemic had recently broken out and spread over the country, so that hardly a day passed without its long journey to perform and deathbed to attend. Often during those days, worn out with fatigue and want of sleep, I would dismount from my mule and rest for a season against a rock or tree, wishing for death to come and release me from so sad an existence.

When I left Montero's house I charged him to send me news of Marta as soon as they should find her; but for several days I heard nothing. At length word came that they had discovered her hiding-place in the forest, but could not induce her to leave it, or even to speak to them; and they implored me to go to them, for they were greatly troubled at her state, and knew not what to do.

Once more I went out to seek her; and this was the saddest journey of all, for even the elements were charged with unusual gloom, as if to prepare my mind for some unimaginable calamity. Rain, accompanied by terrific thunder and lightning, had been falling in torrents for several days, so that the country was all but impassable: the swollen streams roared between the hills, dragging down rocks and trees, and threatening, whenever we were compelled to ford them, to carry us away to destruction. The rain had ceased, but the whole sky was covered by a dark motionless cloud, unpierced by a single ray of sunshine. The mountains, wrapped in blue vapours, loomed before us, vast and desolate; and the trees, in that still, thick atmosphere, were like figures of trees hewn out of solid ink-black rock and set up in some shadowy subterranean region to mock its inhabitants with an imitation of the upper world.

At length we reached Montero's hut, and, followed by all the family, went to look for Marta. The place where she had concealed herself was in a dense wood half a league from the house, and the ascent to it being steep and difficult, Montero was compelled to walk before, leading my mule by the bridle. At length we came to the spot where they had discovered her, and there, in the shadow of the woods, we found Marta still in the same place, seated on the trunk of a fallen tree, which was sodden with the rain and half buried under great creepers and masses of dead and rotting foliage. She was in a crouching attitude, her feet gathered under her garments, which were now torn to rags and fouled with clay; her elbows were planted on her drawn-up knees, and her long bony fingers thrust into her hair, which fell in tangled disorder over her face. To this pitiable condition had she been brought by great and unmerited sufferings.

Seeing her, a cry of compassion escaped my lips, and casting myself off my mule I advanced towards her. As I approached she raised her eyes to mine, and then I stood still, transfixed with amazement and horror at what I saw; for they were no longer those soft violet orbs which had retained until recently their sweet pathetic expression; now they were round and wild-looking, opened to thrice their ordinary size, and filled with a lurid yellow fire, giving them a resemblance to the eyes of some hunted savage animal.

"Great God, she has lost her reason!" I cried; then falling on my knees I disengaged the crucifix from my neck with trembling hands, and endeavoured to hold it up before her sight. This movement appeared to infuriate her; the insane, desolate eyes, from which all human expression had vanished, became like two burning balls, which seemed to shoot out sparks of fire; her short hair rose up until it stood like an immense crest on her head; and suddenly bringing down her skeleton-like hands she thrust the crucifix violently from her, uttering at the same time a succession of moans and cries that pierced my heart with pain to hear. And presently flinging up her arms, she burst forth into shrieks so terrible in the depth of agony they expressed that overcome by the sound I sank upon the earth and hid my face. The others, who were close behind me, did likewise, for no human soul could endure those cries, the remembrance of which, even now after many years, causes the blood to run cold in my veins.

"The Kakué! The Kakué!" exclaimed Montero, who was close behind me.

Recalled to myself by these words I raised my eyes only to discover that Marta was no longer before me. For even in that moment, when those terrible cries were ringing through my heart, waking the echoes of the mountain solitudes, the awful change had come, and she had looked her last with human eyes on earth and on man! In another form—that strange form of the Kakué—she had fled out of our sight for ever to hide in those gloomy woods which were henceforth to be her dwelling place. And I—most miserable of men, what had I done that all my prayers and strivings had been thus frustrated, that out of my very hands the spirit of the power of darkness had thus been permitted to wrest this unhappy soul from me!

I rose up trembling from the earth, the tears pouring unchecked down my cheeks, while the members of Montero's family gathered round me and clung to my garments. Night closed on us, black as despair and death, and with the greatest difficulty we made our way back through the woods. But I would not remain at the rancho; at the risk of my life I returned to Yala, and all through that dark solitary ride I was incessantly crying out to God to have mercy on me. Towards midnight I reached the village in safety, but the horror with which that unheard-of tragedy infected me, the fears and the doubts which dared not yet shape themselves into words, remained in my breast to torture me. For days I could neither eat nor sleep. I was reduced to a skeleton and my hair began to turn white before its time. Being now incapable of performing my duties, and believing that death was approaching I yearned once more for the city of my birth. I escaped at length from Yala, and with great difficulty reached the town of Jujuy, and from hence by slow stages I journeyed back to Cordova.

V

"ONCE more do I behold thee, O Cordova, beautiful to my eyes as the new Jerusalem coming down from Heaven to those who have witnessed the resurrection! Here, where my life began, may I now be allowed to lie down in peace, like a tired child that falls asleep on its mother's breast."

Thus did I apostrophize my natal city, when, looking from the height above, I at last saw it before me, girdled with purple hills and bright with the sunshine, the white towers of the many churches springing out of the green mist of groves and gardens.

Nevertheless Providence ordained that in Cordova I was to find life and not death. Surrounded by old beloved friends, worshipping in the old church I knew so well, health returned to me, and I was like one who rises after a night of evil dreams and goes forth to feel the sunshine and fresh wind on his face. I told the strange story of Marta to one person only; this was Father Irala, a learned and

discreet man of great piety, and one high in
authority in the church at Cordova. I was
astonished that he was able to listen calmly
to the things I related; he spoke some consol-
ing words, but made no attempt then or afterwards to throw any light on the mystery. In
Cordova a great cloud seemed to be lifted from
my mind which left my faith unimpaired; I
was once more cheerful and happy—happier
than I had ever been since leaving it. Three
months went by; then Irala told me one day
that it was time for me to return to Yala, for
my health being restored there was nothing to
keep me longer from my flock.

O that flock, that flock, in which for me
there had been only one precious lamb!

I was greatly disquieted; all those nameless
doubts and fears which had left me now
seemed returning; I begged him to spare me,
to send some younger man, ignorant of the
matters I had imparted to him, to take my
place. He replied that for the very reason
that I was acquainted with those matters I
was the only fit person to go to Yala. Then
in my agitation I unburdened my heart to him.
I spoke of that heathenish apathy of the people I had struggled in vain to overcome, of

the temptations I had encountered—the passion of anger and earthly love, the impulse to commit some terrible crime. Then had come the tragedy of Marta Riquelme, and the spiritual world had seemed to resolve itself into a chaos where Christ was powerless to save; in my misery and despair my reason had almost forsaken me and I had fled from the country. In Cordova hope had revived, my prayers had brought an immediate response, and the Author of salvation seemed to be near to me. Here in Cordova, I said in conclusion, was life, but in the soul-destroying atmosphere of Yala death eternal.

"Brother Sepulvida," he answered, "we know all your sufferings and suffer with you; nevertheless you must return to Yala. Though there in the enemy's country, in the midst of the fight, when hard pressed and wounded, you have perhaps doubted God's omnipotence, He calls you to the front again, where He will be with you and fight at your side. It is for you, not for us, to find the solution of those mysteries which have troubled you; and that you have already come near to the solution your own words seem to show. Remember that we are here not for our own pleasure, but to do our Master's work; that the highest reward will not be for those who sit in the cool shade, book in hand, but for the toilers in the field who are suffering the burden and heat of the day. Return to Yala and be of good heart, and in due time all things will be made clear to your understanding."

These words gave me some comfort, and meditating much on them I took my departure from Cordova, and in due time arrived at my destination.

I had, on quitting Yala, forbidden Montero and his wife to speak of the manner of Marta's disappearance, believing that it would be better for my people to remain in ignorance of such a matter; but now, when going about in the village on my return I found that it was known to every one. That "Marta had become a Kakué," was mentioned on all sides; yet it did not affect them with astonishment and dismay that this should be so, it was merely an event for idle women to chatter about, like Quiteria's elopement or Maxima's quarrel with her mother-in-law.

It was now the hottest season of the year, when it was impossible to be very active, or

much out of doors. During those days the
feeling of despondence began again to weigh
heavily on my heart. I pondered on Irala's
words, and prayed continually, but the illumi-
nation he had prophesied came not. When I
preached, my voice was like the buzzing of
summer flies to the people: they came or sat
or knelt on the floor of the church, and heard
me with stolid unmoved countenances, then
went forth again unchanged in heart. After
the morning Mass I would return to my house,
and, sitting alone in my room, pass the sultry
hours, immersed in melancholy thoughts, having no inclination to work. At such times the
image of Marta, in all the beauty of her girlhood, crowned with her shining golden hair,
would rise before me, until the tears gathering
in my eyes would trickle through my fingers.
Then too I often recalled that terrible scene
in the wood—the crouching figure in its sordid
rags, the glaring furious eyes,—again those
piercing shrieks seemed to ring through me,
and fill the dark mountain's forest with echoes,
and I would start up half maddened with the
sensations of horror renewed within me.

And one day, while sitting in my room, with
these memories for only company, all at once

a voice in my soul told me that the end was approaching, that the crisis was come, and that to whichever side I fell, there I should remain through all eternity. I rose up from my seat staring straight before me, like one who sees an assassin enter his apartment dagger in hand and who nerves himself for the coming struggle. Instantly all my doubts, my fears, my unshapen thoughts found expression, and with a million tongues shrieked out in my soul against my Redeemer. I called aloud on Him to save me, but He came not; and the spirits of darkness, enraged at my long resistance, had violently seized on my soul, and were dragging it down to perdition. I reached forth my hands and took hold of the crucifix standing near me, and clung to it as a drowning mariner does to a floating spar. "Cast it down!" cried out a hundred devils in my ear. "Trample under foot this symbol of a slavery which has darkened your life and made earth a hell! He that died on the cross is powerless now; miserably do they perish who put their trust in Him! Remember Marta Riquelme, and save yourself from her fate while there is time."

My hands relaxed their hold on the cross,

and falling on the stones, I cried aloud to the Lord to slay me and take my soul, for by death only could I escape from that great crime my enemies were urging me to commit.

Scarcely had I pronounced these words before I felt that the fiends had left me, like ravening wolves scared from their quarry. I rose up and washed the blood from my bruised forehead, and praised God; for now there was a great calm in my heart, and I knew that He who died to save the world was with me, and that His grace had enabled me to conquer and deliver my own soul from perdition.

From that time I began to see the meaning of Irala's words, that it was for me and not for him to find the solution of the mysteries which had troubled me, and that I had already come near to finding it. I also saw the reason of that sullen resistance to religion in the minds of the people of Yala; of the temptations which had assailed me—the strange tempests of anger and the carnal passions, never experienced elsewhere, and which had blown upon my heart like hot blighting winds; and even of all the events of Marta Riquelme's tragic life; for all these things had been ordered with devilish cunning to drive my soul into rebellion. I no longer dwelt persistently on that isolated event of her transformation, for now the whole action of that tremendous warfare in which the powers of darkness are arrayed against the messengers of the Gospel began to unfold itself before me.

In thought I went back to the time, centuries ago, when as yet not one ray of heavenly light had fallen upon this continent; when men bowed down in worship to gods, which they called in their several languages Pachacamac, Viracocho, and many others; names which being translated mean, The All-powerful, Ruler of Men, The Strong Comer, Lord of the Dead, The Avenger. These were not mythical beings; they were mighty spiritual entities, differing from each other in character, some taking delight in wars and destruction, while others regarded their human worshippers with tolerant and even kindly feelings. And because of this belief in powerful benevolent beings some learned Christian writers have held that the aborigines possessed a knowledge of the true God, albeit obscured by many false notions. This is a manifest error; for if in the material world light and darkness cannot mingle, much less can the

Supreme Ruler stoop to share His sovereignty
with Belial and Moloch, or in this continent,
with Soychú, Tupa, and Viracocho: but all
these demons, great and small, known by various names, were angels of darkness who had
divided amongst themselves this new world
and the nations dwelling in it.   Nor need we
be astonished at finding here resemblance
to the true religion—majestic and graceful
touches suggesting the Divine Artist; for Satan
himself is clothed as an angel of light, and
scruples not to borrow the things invented
by the Divine Intelligence.   These spirits
possessed unlimited power and authority;
their service was the one great business of all
men's lives; individual character and natural
feelings were crushed out by an implacable
despotism, and no person dreamed of dis-
obedience to their decrees, interpreted by their
high priests; but all men were engaged in raising colossal temples, enriched with gold and
precious stones, to their honour, and priests
and virgins in tens of thousands conducted
their worship with a pomp and magnificence
surpassing those of ancient Egypt or Babylon.
Nor can we doubt that these beings often made
use of their power to suspend the order of na-

ture, transforming men into birds and beasts, causing the trembling of the earth which ruins whole cities, and performing many other stupendous miracles to demonstrate their authority or satisfy their malignant natures. The time came when it pleased the Ruler of the world to overthrow this evil empire, using for that end the ancient, feeble instruments despised of men, the missionary priests, and chiefly those of the often persecuted Brotherhood founded by Loyola, whose zeal and holiness have always been an offence to the proud and carnal-minded. Country after country, tribe after tribe, the old gods were deprived of their kingdom, fighting always with all their weapons to keep back the tide of conquest. And at length, defeated at all points, and like an army fighting in defence of its territory, and gradually retiring before the invader to concentrate itself in some apparently inaccessible region and there stubbornly resist to the end; so have all the old gods and demons retired into this secluded country, where, if they cannot keep out the seeds of truth they have at least succeeded in rendering the soil it falls upon barren as stone. Nor does it seem altogether strange that these once potent beings should be satisfied to remain in comparative obscurity and inaction when the entire globe is open to them, offering fields worthy of their evil ambition. For great as their power and intelligence must be they are, nevertheless, finite beings, possessing, like man, individual characteristics, capabilities and limitations; and after reigning where they have lost a continent, they may possibly be unfit or unwilling to serve elsewhere. For we know that even in the strong places of Christianity there are spirits enough for the evil work of leading men astray; whole nations are given up to damnable heresies, and all religion is trodden under foot by many whose portion will be where the worm dieth not and the fire is not quenched.

From the moment of my last struggle, when this revelation began to dawn upon my mind, I have been safe from their persecutions. No angry passions, no sinful motions, no doubts and despondence disturb the peace of my soul. I was filled with fresh zeal, and in the pulpit felt that it was not my voice, but the voice of some mighty spirit speaking with my lips and preaching to the people with an eloquence of which I was not capable. So far, however, it has been powerless to win their souls. The old gods, although no longer worshipped openly, are their gods still, and could a new Tupǎc Amarǔ arise to pluck down the symbols of Christianity, and proclaim once more the Empire of the Sun, men would everywhere bow down to worship his rising beams and joyfully rebuild temples to the Lightning and the Rainbow.

Although the lost spirits cannot harm they are always near me, watching all my movements, ever striving to frustrate my designs. Nor am I unmindful of their presence. Even here, sitting in my study and looking out on the mountains, rising like stupendous stairs towards heaven and losing their summits in the gathering clouds, I seem to discern the awful shadowy form of Pachacamac, supreme among the old gods. Though his temples are in ruins, where the Pharaohs of the Andes and their millions of slaves worshipped him for a thousand years, he is awful still in his majesty and wrath that plays like lightning on his furrowed brows, kindling his stern countenance, and the beard which rolls downward like an immense white cloud to his knees. Around him gather other tremendous forms in their cloudy vestments—the Strongcomer, the Lord of the Dead, the Avenger, the Ruler of men, and many others whose names were once mighty throughout the continent. They have met to take counsel together; I hear their voices in the thunder hoarsely rolling from the hills, and in the wind stirring the forest before the coming tempest. Their faces are towards me, they are pointing to me with their cloudy hands, they are speaking of me—even of me, an old, feeble, worn-out man! But I do not quail before them; my soul is firm though my flesh is weak; though my knees tremble while I gaze, I dare look forward even to win another victory over them before I depart.

Day and night I pray for that soul still wandering lost in the great wilderness; and no voice rebukes my hope or tells me that my prayer is unlawful. I strain my eyes gazing out towards the forest; but I know not whether Marta Riquelme will return to me with the tidings of her salvation in a dream of the night, or clothed in the garments of the flesh, in the full light of day. For her salvation I wait, and when I have seen it I shall be ready to depart; for as the traveller, whose lips are baked with hot winds, and who thirsts for a cooling draught and swallows sand, strains his eyeballs to see the end of his journey in some great desert, so do I look forward to the goal of this life, when I shall go to Thee, O my Master, and be at rest!

TECLA AND THE LITTLE MEN

TECLA AND THE LITTLE MEN

A LEGEND OF LA PLATA

It happened ninety years ago.
Hard by the spot where I was born,
The tragedy of little Tecla:
Scarce half-a-dozen hoary men
Now the maiden's name remember.
The world has changed, these ancients say,
From what it was;—the plume-like grass
That waved so high, the ostrich blue,
The wild horse and the antlered deer
Are now no more.
Here where the plain
Looks on the level marsh and out
Upon the waters of the Plata
An old estancia house once stood:
And I have played upon its site
In boyhood long ago, and traced
'Mong flowering weeds its old foundations.
'Twas here lived Lara and his wife
With their grown-up sons and daughters;

Happy and rich in pasture lands
And in their numerous herds and flocks.
Before the house a level plain
Bestrewn with shells spread shining white;
And often when the moon was up
Here came a troop of Little Men,
No taller than a boy of twelve,
Robust of limb and long of hair,
And wearing cloaks and broad sombreros.
From windows and from open doors
Distinctly could all see and hear them,
Sitting upon the ground in groups,
In shrill excited voices talking;
Or running to and fro; or ranged
Like cricketers about a field,
Playing their games the whole night long.
But if one ventured from the house
To walk upon their chosen field.
Straightway would they quit their game
To chase him back with hooting shrill,
Hurling showers of stones and pebbles
That rattled on the doors and roof
Like hail, and frightened those within.
Of all in Lara's house but one,
Light-hearted Tecla, feared them not.
The youngest of the daughters she,
A little maiden of fifteen,

Winsome in her wayward moods;
Her blithesomeness and beauty made
Perpetual sunshine in the house.
O merrily would Tecla laugh
When pebbles rattled on the door
To see her bearded brothers start,
And mother and sisters wax so pale,
And oft in pure capriciousness
Alone she'd venture forth to sit
A stone's throw from the gate, just on
The margin of that moonlit field;
There in the twilight would she linger
And bravely watch them by the hour,
Standing or running to and fro,
Hailing each other at their sport.

But once, one evening, trembling, pale,
Flying like a fawn pursued
By leaping hounds, flew Tecla home;
In at the open door she rushed
And clasped her mother close, and then
Crept silently away, and in
A corner sobbed herself to rest:
She would not tell what frightened her,
But from that evening nevermore
Would Tecla venture out alone,
When sunset left the world in shadow.

A month went by; then it was seen
A change had fallen on her spirits;
She was no more the merry one—
The bird that warbled all day long:
Infrequent fell her silvery laugh;
And silent, pale, with faltering steps,
And downcast eyes, she paced the floors,
Who yesterday from room to room
Danced fairylike her blithesome measures.

"O say what ails you, daughter mine?
Imposthumes hidden, spasms, rheums,
Catarrhs and wasting calentures,
Have yielded to the juices I
Express from herbs medicinal;
Yet this most subtle malady
Still mocks your mother's love and skill."
"I have no sickness, mother, 'tis
But weakness; for I cannot eat,
Since on one day, long weeks ago,
Each morsel all at once appeared,
Even as I raised it, red with dust,
And thus till now it is with me;
And water limpid from the well,
And milk, grow turbid with red dust
When lifted to my thirsting lips,
Until I loathe all aliment."

" 'Tis but a sickly fancy, child,
Born of a weak distempered stomach
That can no longer bear strong food.
But you shall have things delicate
And easy to digest; the stream
Shall give its little silvery fish
To tempt; the marsh its painted eggs
Of snipe and dotterel; sweet curds
Made fragrant with the purple juice
Of thistle bloom I'll make for you
Each day, until the yellow root
Of the wild red vinegar-flower,
With powders made from gizards dried
Of iron-eating ostriches
Bring back a healthy appetite.
And make your nostrils love again
The steam of roasted armadillo."

Vain was her skill: no virtue dwelt
The wasting maiden to restore
In powders or in root.   And soon
The failing footsteps ceased their rounds,
And through the long, long summer days
Her white cheek rested on her pillow.
And often when the moonlight shone
Upon her bed, she, lying still,
Would listen to the plover's cry,

And tinkling of the bell-mare's bell,
Come faintly from the dreamy distance;
Then in her wistful eyes would shine
A light that made her mother weep.

Within the wide old kitchen once
The Laras from their evening meal
Were startled by a piercing cry
From Tecla's room; and rushing in
They found her sobbing on the floor,
Trembling, as white as any ghost.
They lifted her—O easy 'twas
To lift her now, for she was light
As pining egret in their arms,
And laid her on her bed.   And when
Her terror left her, and the balm
They gave had soothed her throbbing
      heart,
Clasped in her mother's arms she told
The story of her malady.

"Do you remember, mother mine,
How once with terror palpitating
Into the house I ran?   That eve
Long had I sat beyond the gate
Listening to the shrill-voiced talking
And laughter of the Little People,

And half I wished—oh, was it wrong?
Yet feared to join them in their games.
When suddenly on my neck I felt
A clasping arm, and in my ear
A voice that whispered—'Tecla sweet,
A valiant little maid art thou!'
O mother, 'twas a Little Man,
And through the grass and herbage tall,
Soft stealing like a cat, he came,
And leaped upon the stone, and sat
By me! I rose and ran away;
Then fast he followed, crying out,
'Run; tell your mother you have found
A lover who will come full soon
For thee; run, run, thy sisters tell
Thou hast a lover rich in gold
And gems to make them pine with envy!'
And he has caused this weakness, mother;
And often when I lie awake
He comes to peer in at the window,
And smiles and whispers pretty things.
This night he came, and at my side,
Wearing a cloak all beautiful
With scarlet bright embroidery,
He sat and boldly played the lover."

"And what said he? The wicked imp!"

"He asked me if that yellow root
That's bitter to the taste, and all
My wise old mother's medicines
Had made me hungry.   Then he held
A golden berry to my mouth—
The fruitlet of the Camambù:
O beautiful it looked, and had
No red or grimy dust upon it!
And when I ate and found it sweet,
And asked with hungry tears for more,
He whispered pleasant promises
Of honied fruits: and then he spoke—
O mother mine, what did he mean!—
Of wanderings over all the earth,
Lit by the moon, above the dim
Vast forests; over tumbling waves,
And hills that soar beyond the clouds.
Then eagerly I started up
For joy to fly away with him
Bird-like above the world, to seek
Green realms; and in his arms he clasped
And raised me from my bed.   But soon
As from a dream I screaming woke,
And strove so strongly to be free
He dropped me on the floor and fled."

"O daughter dear, how narrowly
Hast 'scaped! But not to you again
Shall come such moments perilous;
For know, O Tecla, and rejoice
That from this moment dates your cure,
Since like a wise physician I
Up to its hidden source have traced
The evil that afflicted you.
In former days the Little Men
Oft played their wicked pranks, but years
Have passed since any proof they gave
Of their malificence, since sharp
And bitter lessons given them
By Holy Church had taught these imps
To know their place; and now I too
Shall draw against them sacred weapons."

Next morning to the Monastery
Hard by, where dwelt a brotherhood
Of Friars Dominican, was sent
A messenger, the holy men
To summon to the house of Lara—
To arm with ghostly arms and free
Fair Tecla from these persecutions.

At noon, wrapped in a dusty cloud,
Six mounted Friars came riding in

Their steeds at furious gallop.   They,
Rough men, spent no ignoble lives
In barren offices; but broke
The steeds they rode, and pastured herds
Of half-wild cattle, wide around
The ostrich and the puma hunted.
Thus boldly came they—Tecla's knights,
Armed with a flask of holy water,
Nor wanting at their leathern girdles
Long knives and pistols with brass barrels.

Forthwith the blest campaign began;
And through the house and round the house
They walked; on windows, walls, and doors
Sprinkling the potent drops that keep
All evil things from entering;
And curses in a learned tongue
They hurled against the Little Men.

O gladly beat the heart within
The breast of every Lara there
For Tecla timely saved!   She too
The sweet infection caught, and blest
With hope and health reviving laughed
The silvery laugh too long unheard.

And there was nothing more to do
Now but to finish day so good

With feast and merriment.　Then lambs
And sucking pigs were straightway slain
To heap the board hospitable;
While screaming over fields and ditches
Turkeys and ducks were chased to make
A rich repast.　Then freely round
Travelled the mighty jugs of wine,
Till supper done the Friar Blas
Snatched the guitar: "Away," he cried,
"With chairs and tables!　Let us show
The daughters of the house of Lara
That our most holy monastery
Can give them partners for the dance!"

Loudly the contra-dance he played,
And sang, while standing in two rows
The ready dancers ranged themselves;
Till on her pillow Tecla smiled
To hear the strings twang merrily:
"O hasten, mother mine," she cried,
"To join the dance, and open wide
The doors so that the sounds may reach
　　me."

And while they danced the Friar Blas
Improvised merry boastful words,
And couplets full of laughing jibes:—

"Dost know how to sing, Little Man?
Come sing with a Dominican.

"O when I remember our fight
I must laugh for my victory tonight.

"There conquered you bleed and repine;
Here sing I and drink the red wine.

"I'll preach you a sermon in song—
My sermons are merry not long.

"No more to sweet Tecla aspire,
For know that your rival's a Friar.

"Not wise was your wooing, but cruel,
For who can have fire without fuel?

"Did'st lose her by making her thin?
By fattening perchance I shall win.

"For when the pale maiden gets well
I'll carry her off to my cell;

"For the labourer he looks for his hire,
And hot is the heart of the Friar."

A burst of laughter and applause
Followed the strain. Out rung a peal
Of eldritch laughter echoing theirs!
Sitting and standing, dancers clasped
In joyous attitudes, transfixed,
All silent, motionless, amazed,
They listened as it louder grew—
That laughter demoniacal—
Till jugs and glasses jingled loud
Upon the table, as when hoarse
Deep thunder rumbles near, and doors
And windows shudder in their frames,
And all the solid house is shaken
To its foundations. Slowly it died;
But even as it died they heard
A wailing cry:—far off it seemed,
Still ever growing more remote,
Until they thought 'twas but the sound
The stringed guitar, dropped on the floor,
Gave forth, upon their straining ears
Slow dying in long reverberations.
Up sprang the mother suddenly
Giving a mighty cry, and flew
To Tecla's chamber. After her
The others trooped, and found her there
Weeping beside the empty cot,
Wringing her hands and wailing loud

Calling on Tecla gone for ever.
In at the open window blew
The fresh night wind; and forth they peered
With straining eyes and faces white,
Their hearts with strange surmisings filled.
Only the moon they saw, ghost-like
In heaven walking: 'neath its light
Immeasurable spread the marsh,
And far off shone the sea-like river;
Only the swelling waves they heard,
Low murmuring to their listening ears
Through the deep silence of the night.

APPENDIX TO EL OMBÚ

APPENDIX TO EL OMBÚ.

THE ENGLISH INVASION AND THE GAME OF EL PATO

I MUST say at once that El Ombú is mostly a true story, although the events did not occur exactly in the order given. The incidents relating to the English invasion of June and July, 1807, is told pretty much as I had it from the old gaucho called Nicandro in the narrative. That was in the sixties. The undated notes which I made of my talks with the old man, containing numerous anecdotes of Santos Ugarte and the whole history of El Ombú, were written, I think, in 1868—the year of the great dust storm. These ancient notes are now before me, and look very strange, both as to the writing and the quality of the paper; also as to the dirtiness of the same, which makes me think that the old manuscript must have been out in that memorable storm, which, I remember, ended with rain—the rain coming down as liquid mud.

There were other old men living in that part of the country who, as boys, had witnessed the march of an English army on Buenos Ayres, and one of these confirmed the story of the blankets thrown away by the army, and of the chaff between some of the British soldiers and the natives.

I confess I had some doubts as to the truth of this blanket story when I came to read over my old notes; but in referring to the proceedings of the court-martial on Lieutenant-General Whitelocke, published in London in 1808, I find that the incident is referred to. On page 57 of the first volume occurs the following statement, made by General Gower in his evidence. "The men, particularly of Brigadier-General Lumley's brigade, were very much exhausted, and Lieutenant-General Whitelocke, to give them a chance of getting on with tolerable rapidity, ordered all the blankets of the army to be thrown down."

There is nothing, however, in the evidence about the blankets having been used to make a firmer bottom for the army to cross a river, nor is the name of the river mentioned.

Another point in the old gaucho's story may

strike the English reader as very strange and
almost incredible; this is, that within a very
few miles of the army of the hated foreign invader, during its march on the capital, where
the greatest excitement prevailed and every
preparation for defence was being made, a
large number of men were amusing themselves
at the game of El Pato.   To those who are acquainted with the character of the gaucho
there is nothing incredible in such a fact; for
the gaucho is, or was, absolutely devoid of the
sentiment of patriotism, and regarded all
rulers, all in authority from the highest to the
lowest, as his chief enemies, and the worst kind
of robbers, since they robbed him not only of
his goods but of his liberty.

It mattered not to him whether his country
paid tribute to Spain or to England, whether
a man appointed by some one at a distance as
Governor or Viceroy had black or blue eyes.
It was seen that when the Spanish dominion
came to an end his hatred was transferred to
the ruling cliques of a so-called Republic.
When the gauchos attached themselves to
Rosas, and assisted him to climb into power,
they were under the delusion that he was one
of themselves, and would give them that per-

fect liberty to live their own lives in their own way, which is their only desire. They found out their mistake when it was too late.

It was Rosas who abolished the game of El Pato, but before saying more on that point it would be best to describe the game. I have never seen an account of it in print, but for a very long period, and down to probably about 1840, it was the most popular out-door game on the Argentine pampas. Doubtless it originated there; it was certainly admirably suited to the habits and disposition of the horsemen of the plains; and unlike most out-door games it retained its original simple, rude character to the end.

Pato means duck; and to play the game a duck or fowl, or, as was usually the case, some larger domestic bird—turkey, gosling, or muscovy duck—was killed and sewn up in a piece of stout raw hide, forming a somewhat shapeless ball, twice as big as a football, and provided with four loops or handles of strong twisted raw hide made of a convenient size to be grasped by a man's hand. A great point was to have the ball and handles so strongly made that three or four powerful men could take hold and tug until they dragged each other to the ground without anything giving way.

Whenever it was resolved at any place to have a game, and someone had offered to provide the bird, and the meeting place had been settled, notice would be sent round among the neighbours; and at the appointed time all the men and youths living within a circle of several leagues would appear on the spot, mounted on their best horses. On the appearance of the man on the ground carrying the duck the others would give chase; and by-and-by he would be overtaken, and the ball wrested from his hand; the victor in his turn would be pursued, and when overtaken there would perhaps be a scuffle or scrimmage, as in football, only the strugglers would be first on horseback before dragging each other to the earth. Occasionally when this happened a couple of hot-headed players, angry at being hurt or worsted, would draw their weapons against each other in order to find who was in the right, or to prove which was the better man. But fight or no fight, some one would get the duck and carry it away to be chased again. Leagues of ground would be gone over by the players in this way, and at last some one, luckier or better mounted than his fellows, would get the duck and successfully run the gauntlet of the people scattered about on the plain, and make good his escape. He was the victor, and it was his right to carry the bird home and have it for his dinner. This was, however, a mere fiction; the man who carried off the duck made for the nearest house, followed by all the others, and there not only the duck was cooked, but a vast amount of meat to feed the whole of the players. While the dinner was in preparation, messengers would be despatched to neighbouring houses to invite the women; and on their arrival dancing would be started and kept up all night.

To the gauchos of the great plains, who took to the back of a horse from childhood, almost as spontaneously as a parasite to the animal on which it feeds, the Pato was the game of games, and in their country as much as cricket and football and golf together to the inhabitants of this island. Nor could there have been any better game for men whose existence, or whose success in life, depended so much on their horsemanship; and whose chief glory it was to be able to stick on under difficulties, and, when sticking on was impossible, to fall off gracefully and, like a cat, on their feet. To this game the people of the pampas were devoted up to a time when it came into the head of a president of the republic to have no more of it, and with a stroke of the pen it was abolished for ever.

It would take a strong man in this country to put down any out-door game to which the people are attached; and he was assuredly a very strong man who did away with El Pato in that land. If any other man who has occupied the position of head of the State at any time during the last ninety years, had attempted such a thing a universal shout of derision would have been the result, and wherever such an absurd decree had appeared pasted up on the walls and doors of churches, shops, and other public places, the gauchos would have been seen filling their mouths with water to squirt it over the despised paper. But this man was more than a president; he was that Rosas, called by his enemies the "Nero of America." Though by birth a member of a distinguished family, he was by predilection a gaucho, and early in life took to the semibarbarous life of the plains. Among his fellows Rosas distinguished himself as a dare-devil, one who was not afraid to throw himself from the back of his own horse on to that of a wild horse in the midst of a flying herd into which he had charged. He had all the gaucho's native ferocity, his fierce hates and prejudices; and it was in fact his intimate knowledge of the people he lived with, his oneness in mind with them, that gave him his wonderful influence over them, and enabled him to carry out his ambitious schemes. But why, when he had succeeded in making himself all-powerful by means of their help, when he owed them so much, and the ties uniting him to them were so close, did he deprive them of their beloved pastime? The reason, which will sound almost ridiculous after what I have said of the man's character, was that he considered the game too rough. It is true that it had (for him) its advantages, since it made the men of the plains hardy, daring, resourceful fighters on horseback—the kind of men he most needed for his wars; on the other hand, it caused so much injury to the players, and resulted in so many bloody fights and fierce feuds between neighbours that he considered he lost more than he gained by it.

There were not men enough in the country for his wants; even boys of twelve and fourteen were sometimes torn from the arms of their weeping mothers to be made soldiers of; he could not afford to have full-grown strong men injuring and killing each other for their own amusement. They must, like good citizens, sacrifice their pleasure for their country's sake. And at length, when his twenty years' reign was over, when people were again free to follow their own inclinations without fear of bullet and cold steel—it was generally cold steel in those days—those who had previously played the game had had roughness enough in their lives, and now only wanted rest and ease; while the young men and youths who had not taken part in El Pato nor seen it played, had never come under its fascination, and had no wish to see it revived.

THE END